Praise for *Atchafalaya Darling*:

"There's so much tenderness in these stories, all wrapped in vibrantly bubbling scenes and conversations. Dasgupta cares about all these characters and it shows all over the pages and pulls a reader in."

—Aimee Bender, author of *The Girl in the Flammable Skirt*
and *The Butterfly Lampshade*

Praise for *Histories of Memories*:

"In the vulnerable, gorgeously written, and brilliantly illustrated *Histories of Memories*, Shome Dasgupta offers the reader an unflinching account of love and loss, failure and redemption, pleasure and pain. Dasgupta layers locations—Kolkata, Edmonton, Munich—with soundtracks—*Dr. Dolittle*, *The Perks of Being a Wallflower*, *Magnolia*—and family—mother, father, uncle, brother, with friends, lifelong and long gone: a mixtape filled with his distinctive lyricism."

—Melissa Llanes Brownlee, author of *Hard Skin*
and *Kahi and Lua*

"Page by page, these stories transport, restore, nourish, and remind. They bring us chocolates and curries, mud and family, songs and sights from all over the planet. More than anything, they show us humanity. And for that, for this author, I am truly grateful."

—Jack B. Bedell, Poet Laureate of Louisiana, 2017–2019

"Shome Dasgupta charts a sometimes surreal and always beautiful crossing of time and space . . . . The past is always accessible, even as it shapeshifts on the altars of remembrance. Dasgupta reveals the radiant potentials of short form storytelling."

—Ra'Niqua Lee, author of *For What Ails You*

ATCHAFALAYA
DARLING

ATCHAFALAYA DARLING

STORIES

SHOME DASGUPTA

Fort Smith, Arkansas

ATCHAFALAYA DARLING

Edited by Casie Dodd
Cover image: Theo van Hoytema (detail, *Zes kikkers en padden*),
   The Rijksmuseum

Belle Point Press, LLC
Fort Smith, Arkansas
bellepointpress.com
editor@bellepointpress.com

Find Belle Point Press
on Facebook, Substack,
and Instagram (@bellepointpress)

Printed in the United States of America

28 27 26 25 24   1 2 3 4 5

Library of Congress Control Number: 2024937361

ISBN: 978-1-960215-19-2

ATCH/BPP30

for Katie

Contents

A Familiar Frottoir

A DIFFERENT KIND of sunlight that day—the day Bisque sat out on the stoop, shucking pistachios, and the gleam of the air settled in on his face, casting half a shadow, a shadow full of cracked thoughts and known uncertainties. The day itself sounded like a broken nose—an incessant buzz, a wiry hum, and this was his mood as he split pistachios, tossing them into an orange bucket, keeping the papery flakes for himself, sucking each shell like oysters.

Grandmother Violon was dying, this Bisque knew—bedridden for the past four months in the loft upstairs of Bisque's house in St. Martinville, once a church. The stained-glass windows were still there—the scent of oak and candle wax stitched in its history since 1904—and Bisque had moved into the church eight years ago, after the last prayer was hummed by its people.

Here's the steeple, he thought as the sun was slanted—a bent horizon, one eye closed while picking away at the pistachios—the only attraction to Grandmother Violon these days, the particular texture after the first chew was what she enjoyed most as they tumbled around on her tongue. Other than Bisque, who had been taking care of her for eleven years, her only memory of joy was pistachios. Bisque himself enjoyed David's Bar-B-Q-flavored sunflower seeds but had taken a liking to the flakes coating the shells which now became his way of thinking, allowing him to focus on the day's entries—whether past, present, or future.

He chucked the last pistachio of the bag into the orange bucket and tilted his head, still one eye closed, and watched the world wobble a bit before going back inside.

"Mémère," Bisque called out.

He walked up the stairs, which creaked with every step, and with each step he would imagine the case breaking in and falling down into the core of the earth where the faint music of an accordion playing in the distance could be heard as he danced the two-step around molten metal—this time, there was also a frottoir rattling away, and the sound remained in his head after snapping out of his reverie. He pressed his tongue to the roof of his mouth, tasting the last of the flakes. He saw Grandmother Violon in her bed. The rattling stopped.

"I'm here, Mémère."

"Cher," Grandmother Violon said, "there are no ghosts."

She was on her side, facing the door—Bisque had positioned her that way so that she could see him walk up the stairs.

"Where are the ghosts, Mémère?" he replied.

"There are no ghosts."

Bisque gently put his arms around her, setting her back against the headboard of the bed.

"Mémère—I have pistachios."

This was one of only a few words that would make Mémère smile. She put her hand on Bisque's wrist, papery and thin—a slight tremble.

"Have you eaten?" she asked.

"I'm good, Mémère—let's have some pistachios now."

"Cher."

Bisque put the orange bucket down on the wooden floor and sat on the straw chair just next to the bed. He scooped up a handful.

"Have a mouth open, Mémère."

"Yes, cher."

Bisque slowly put a pistachio in her mouth, and Grandmother Violon rolled it around her tongue before chewing. There is life, Bisque thought, as he waited for her to finish. He put another one in her mouth. The light was broken as it came through the stained-glass window, coming in from the other side of the room.

"Here," Bisque said. "I'll put these on for you, Mémère."

He placed a pair of large and round sunglasses around her eyes.

"What do you see, Mémère?"

"I see no ghosts, cher."

"Good."

"How much longer do I have left, petit Bisque?" Grandmother Violon asked.

Her voice was as thin as her wrists—the way the light came in, Bisque could see swirls of rainbow-colored particles in the beam. Beyond the shine, he saw an owl perched on the oak—its eyes coming through. Bisque put his hand on Grandmother Violon's forehead and rubbed her temples with his fingertips.

"Mémère."

He fed her another pistachio.

"I don't think you have too much longer left."

He kissed her on the cheek.

"Bring the ghosts," she said, "and let them take me away."

"They're coming, Mémère—soon. I will miss you, Mémère."

She lifted her arm—too weak to reach its destination, Bisque crouched over and bowed his head to let Grandmother Violon brush her hand through his hair. The simplicity of its touch provided him with comfort—so a series of memories of his youth and his grandmother, energetic and lively, playing horse and carriage in the front yard. Those echoes of the past rippled through his mind, a world where there was no pain, a time when they weren't waiting for any ghosts.

"I know, cher—such good times."

From the bedside table, he poured a glass of water.

"Let's have a few more pistachios, Mémère, and then a bit of water."

"And then the ghosts, cher?"

"Maybe so, Mémère—no more worry, now."

After three more pistachios, Bisque tilted the glass while raising his grandmother's chin—she slowly sipped, each swallow a moment of remembrance for Grandmother Violon.

"You're a dear for taking care of me, petit Bisque, for all this time. I'm happy."

"I'm happy, Mémère—sleep now—I'll be back in just a bit now."

He adjusted her body so that she was flat on the bed and took off her sunglasses. Bisque looked into her eyes—he saw the ghosts in them resembling raccoons on their hinds with their paws in the wind. Through the window, the owl was gone—just a bit more time, he thought, and Grandmother Violon closed her eyes. It didn't take too long for her to sleep, a deep sleep—Bisque listened to her breathe knowing that there would be a time, soon, when there would be no breathing—when her chest would remain still.

Back outside—the evening was still there, the tip of the sun dipping beyond roofs of houses before Bisque as he lay in the grass with the sky staring back at him. Please let it be peaceful, he thought—please take her with ease. I am no one any longer—no one for her. The owl flew over, its wings so wide they enveloped the last of the sun, and there was darkness. The shades around his eyes grew darker as the days took their toll on his way of life. He wouldn't have it any other way though—the love for his grandmother had no bounds or limits.

In came the Gulf winds, pressing against his body, a familiar smell, and as the air lost its light, Bisque saw ashes twirling around, an incessant sound of rustling—he sat himself up. Across the street, there was a house and it was on fire. Mr. Veron, he thought—a neighbor, late in his years who had shown the tricks of life to Bisque, from fixing a broken lawn mower to working the engine of his car. A gentle man with calloused hands and soft eyes—Mr. Veron looked over Bisque as he looked over Grandmother Violon, sometimes bringing over pecan pies and satsumas, or inviting them over for gumbo when it was cold outside—this was when Grandmother was more mobile and active. When she became bedridden, Mr. Veron would instead walk over to their house using a broken branch rasped into a cane, and they would sit in Grandmother Violon's room, dining on shrimp and grits. He'd bring his radio over, and they'd listen to zydeco on KRVS.

Mr. Veron, Bisque thought. It was the roof that was smoking, and Bisque rushed over to his house. The door was open—it was always open—and he ran in, calling out Mr. Veron's name.

"Oh I'm here, good sir," Bisque heard.

He walked into the kitchen, where Mr. Veron was standing at the oven wearing mitts. He wore an apron, and his glasses were tilted as they were missing one of the temples—they had been like that for as long as Bisque knew him.

"I'm just about to finish baking this bread pudding for y'all, Bisque—I'm happy you're here."

Bisque breathed in the kitchen and tasted its air.

"Mr. Veron," he said, "we need to get out and call the fire department."

"Now why is that, good sir?"

"Mr. Veron, your house is on fire. The roof."

"Is that so?"

"It's so, Mr. Veron—let's get."

"Well the bread pudding is just about to finish up here—let me take this over to Grandmother Violon. She might not eat it, but I think she'll like the look of it."

"Mr. Veron—I think we need to get now."

The aroma of the kitchen quickly shifted over to the smell of smoke. The house became dark, and the fire was rustling louder.

Over at the church, Grandmother Violon lay in her bed, facing the stairs. Her eyes were open and she reached out, not knowing what she was reaching out to—she called out, in a faint voice, for Bisque.

"The ghosts," she said. "Cher Bisque—the ghosts. There are no ghosts. Where are the ghosts?"

She lifted her head—so slightly—and turned it, looking at the window, where all she saw was darkness. She continued to talk to herself.

"Seems right. Let them come."

Fiddling with the sunglasses, which had been placed next to her on the bed earlier by Bisque, Grandmother Violon managed to put them on.

"There is light," she said. "Petit Bisque—there is light."

"Let's get, Mr. Veron," Bisque said.

"Sure thing, good sir."

Mr. Veron bent over and pulled out the bread pudding.

"It's hot, but it smells so good."

Bisque grabbed Mr. Veron's walking cane.

"Come on now," Bisque said in a gentle voice. "It certainly smells so good, but let's get."

"Your grandmother will love the way this looks," Mr. Veron said.

Bisque saw the proud twinkle in his eyes—he smiled big, with his remaining teeth showing.

"She sure will," Bisque said. "Let's take that on over to our house and show Grandmother Violon."

"Bon," Mr. Veron replied.

"Mr. Veron," Bisque said, "where are your teeth?"

"Oh I kept them in the living room," he replied. "I guess I'll need them now."

"Hold on."

Bisque went into the living room and saw his teeth on the coffee table, next to a stack of *Southern Living* magazines. There was smoke. He picked up the dentures and put them in his pocket and went back to the kitchen where he saw Mr. Veron looking up, staring at the ceiling.

Bisque took the bread pudding from Mr. Veron and gave him the walking cane. The pan was burning his hand, but he held onto it and gritted his teeth—his other hand on Mr. Veron's arm. The smoke had started to come in as full clouds. They made it outside, where a crowd had already gathered. Step by step, Bisque and Mr. Veron reached the edge of the yard and turned around. One of the neighbors had mentioned that the fire department had been called, and the sirens could be heard in the distance. Bisque put the bread pudding down on the road and rubbed his hands before blowing on them.

"Oh look at that," said Mr. Veron. "Looks like a good fire—good thing we got the bread pudding out."

He patted Bisque on the shoulder.

"You're right about that, Mr. Veron."

"Don't you worry," one of the neighbors said. "We'll take real good care of you."

Mr. Veron nodded and smiled.

"At least we got the bread pudding," he added.

"I'll be right back, Mr. Veron," Bisque said. "Just grab a seat on that chair and wait for the fire department."

He asked one of the neighbors to stay with Mr. Veron.

"What about the bread pudding?" Mr. Veron asked.

"I'll take it inside the church," Bisque replied. "It'll be there waiting for all of us."

The fire truck arrived, and the crowd gave them their space, spreading out across the street. Some asked if they could help. Out came the large hose. Bisque shouted that there was no one inside.

"Such a strange waterfall," Mr. Veron said.

"Here," Bisque said, "look."

He grabbed the chair and put it next to Mr. Veron.

"Have a seat right here—I'll be right back."

"Good sir."

"Here, Mr. Veron—take this."

Bisque handed him the teeth, and Mr. Veron put them in his shirt pocket, tucked under the apron.

The church was dark—Bisque entered holding the bread pudding. There was rattling near the sink. He called out Grandmother Violon's name. The rattling stopped. A streetlight gave way through the window and Bisque looked toward the sink. Ghosts, he thought—there are no ghosts.

"Mémère."

A shadow shifted—outside, he could still hear the people talking and shouting as they stood on the road in front of the house on fire, and the hose was still in full force. Bisque saw a figure—dressed in all black, a face covered in a bandana.

"You can take what you like," Bisque said.

He looked on the counter, where there was only a fork. He reached out to pick it up.

"Don't," the voice said.

Bisque put the bread pudding down on the counter.

"You can take what you like except for the bread pudding—it's not mine," he said.

"It smells good," the voice said.

"I can give you a bit."

There was a pause—the sink rattled again.

"Mémère," Bisque said.

"What's that?"

"My grandmother—Violon."

"Where is she?"

"Upstairs."

"I haven't been upstairs."

The sound of windows breaking came from across the street.

"There's a fire," Bisque said.

"I saw."

"Mémère," Bisque said.

"I won't hurt her. I won't hurt you either if you do nothing wrong."

"Would you like some bread pudding?"

"Is Mr. Veron okay?"

"You know him."

"I do."

"Why?"

"He's a gentleman."

"Now that's right," Bisque said.

"Keep the lights off."

"I will."

"It smells nice in here."

"I need to see Mémère—she's dying."

"I know."

"Are you a ghost?" Bisque asked.

The figure took a few steps back and leaned over—looking out the window, across the street.

"I'm just a guy."

Bisque saw that he was holding a small jewelry box—he had kept it in the living room. Carved in wood and engraved, a family heirloom which Grandmother Violon had passed down to Bisque. He kept nothing in it—Grandmother Violon had given away all of her belongings, keeping only a few sets of clothing.

"That's a nice box there," Bisque said.

"The carvings," the voice said.

Bisque saw him move his hands around the surface of the box.

"It's pretty."

"It belonged to Mémère—it has been in the family for generations."

"It's pretty."

Bisque took a step forward and the figure moved back.

"Would you like it back?" the voice asked.

"Seems fine."

Bisque reached out for the fork. He thought about Grandmother Violon upstairs. The rush of the crowd outside hushed, and the people started going on their way. Bisque could see that Mr. Veron was still outside, sitting in his chair. He quickly moved his hand over to his pocket and patted it. He sighed, remembering that he had already given Mr. Veron his teeth. He reached out for the fork again.

"Please don't," the voice said.

"Speak again."

"What's that?"

Bisque took in a long breath and exhaled.

"Francis," he said. "Francis—is that you?"

"Yes, sir."

"What are you doing?"

"I was just stealing some things."

Bisque switched on the light and saw Francis, dressed in black—his face covered in a blue bandana.

"Hi, Mr. Bisque," Francis said.

"Have a seat."

He pulled out a chair for Francis and then one out for himself.

"Now why are you stealing from me?"

"I saw the fire," Francis replied, "and everyone was there so I thought I'd just duck in over here and pick up some things to sell—but I don't want to sell this box. I just want to keep it and put it in my room. It's pretty."

Bisque looked out the window—Mr. Veron's house looked calm.

"You could've just asked, you know that—right? I mean I can help you out."

"I'm sorry, Mr. Bisque."

Bisque thought about the jewelry box and the generations it had been through—he thought about his grandmother and how her time was nearing.

"You can have the box," Bisque said. "I keep all my memories in the box in my head."

Francis took off his bandana and smiled, thanking him. He reached out his hand.

"Here."

In his palm was a set of earrings—Bisque didn't even know that he had them or where they were kept.

"I was going to give them to my girlfriend," Francis said. "But it's my gift to you—as a thank you."

"Well thank you for giving me back what you stole from me," Bisque said, "as a gift."

"My pleasure, Mr. Bisque. Mr. Bisque—are you going to tell Ma?"

"If I hear about it again, I will—now get."

"Yes, sir."

Francis stuck out his hand, and Bisque shook it.

"Come back next week," Bisque said, "and I'll get you some dinner and dessert."

"Yes, sir."

Francis went out the front door, and Bisque let out a loud sigh, relieved that nothing worse had happened. Just as he was about to head upstairs to check on Grandmother Violon, he heard a call for his name coming from outside—Mr. Veron. He walked over.

"You good," Bisque said.

"Well," Mr. Veron said, "looks like my house caught on fire—you see that."

"I sure do," Bisque said. "Don't you worry—we'll get it all cleaned up and good to go. You can stay at the church in the meantime."

Bisque flinched and looked around as if he had heard a whisper. A strong push of the Gulf breeze came through. Mr. Veron coughed—the smoke still in its trails.

"Let's get inside now," Bisque said.

"I lost the bread pudding," Mr. Veron said.

"It's at the church."

"I lost my teeth."

"They're in your pocket."

Mr. Veron patted his legs, pulled out his teeth—expressing joy as if he had found some money.

"Let's have some of that bread pudding," Bisque said. "How about that?"

Bisque told the fire marshal that they'd be across the street, and they walked back to the church—Bisque poured him a glass of water. The stained-glass windows appeared brighter to Bisque that night, almost alive.

"Just rest for a bit," he said. "Get that tongue ready for some pudding."

Bisque patted Mr. Veron on the shoulder and walked toward the stairs.

"I'm coming up, Mémère."

On the eighth step—as it creaked—Bisque saw himself tumble through toward the core of the earth, a whirring in his ears. In his descent, he traveled through soil and roots, scraping and scratching his body and face, nicking like razors—he grunted as he twirled and twisted. There—among molten metal and magma, he saw a sphere dressed in blue and yellow fire, quietly roaring, calm and comforting. There was no smoke. And there— he saw Grandmother Violon, holding an accordion, a frottoir, fresh and shiny, covering her body. Her appearance—youthful and vibrant and strong—the fire itself reflecting in her eyes, Bisque was hypnotized as he was on his knees before her. Perched on her shoulder—an owl with large wings, a beak so yellow and bright it cast light, making Bisque squint as he tried to gather in his surroundings. A familiar breeze came through—that which he recognized originating from the Gulf—and the flames tossed about in unison, in rhythm. Grandmother Violon played the accordion, tapping her foot against the dirt of the world, her chin up as her voice echoed throughout Bisque's vision. A silence. Beams entering through the pores of the crust, Bisque felt an unfamiliar sensation—only that which he could pin as ghosts circling around him.

"Mémère," Bisque managed to say, just below a whisper.

She heard.

"Petit Bisque."

She spoke in a voice Bisque hadn't heard in years—a voice which recalled a time when they rode horses together and tended to the farm from the morning sun to dusk's awakening. This was a voice now which became infinite. A cow walked behind her, turning its head toward Bisque with a slight tilt.

"The pain," Bisque said.

"Released," Grandmother Violon replied.

The cow now gone—the owl still on her shoulder, head unmoved.

"They've come," Grandmother Violon said. "They've come and took me away with gentility."

"Mémère—there are ghosts," Bisque said.

"There are ghosts," Grandmother Violon said.

"What will I do?"

"The church is your home, cher Bisque—take care of your chores."

"I've never cried," Bisque said.

"Cry and let this world in—let the world take its own through your skin."

She played the accordion—next to her, an orange bucket full of pistachios. The owl lifted, taking the bucket away with its talons—its wings swooped, engulfing Bisque's vision until there was no bird. Gone. The fire, blue and welcoming, continued to gleam in Grandmother Violon's eyes.

"Je t'aime," Grandmother Violon said.

Her voice caused Bisque's realm to tremor.

"Je t'aime—Je t'aime—Je t'aime," she continued.

"Mémère."

"You are needed," she replied. "No longer from me—but for others. You know, cher. Your love will keep them going."

Bisque thought about Francis and Mr. Veron.

"They need you," Grandmother Violon said.

She tapped her foot as if the music was still playing.

"Bring the farm back," she said, "and you'll be there."

"I love you, Mémère."

"Je t'aime, petit Bisque—cher."

With that, Grandmother Violon tossed a packet of David's Bar-B-Q-flavored sunflower seeds to Bisque, and as he grabbed them, he saw Grandmother Violon disappear, a smile which radiated into him. He heard the rattling of the frottoir—a crisp and clear melody, then distant, an echo, and then a familiar hum ending in quiet vibrations. Silence.

"Ghost," he said.

His own voice now, booming and echoing. He stood and took a step and found himself leaning on the banister of the staircase, at the top— before him lay Grandmother Violon, on her side. Her sunglasses rested on her body, and when Bisque looked at her, he saw what appeared to be a smile on her face. Her eyes were closed.

Bisque slowly walked toward her, looking around, making sure that he was at the church. He knelt at the bedside and looked at his grandmother, taking in a deep breath and letting go. Outside the window, the branches were bare in the dark. The glass of water on the table was empty, and Grandmother Violon's hands were clasped, tucked under the side of her face, as if she was having a beautiful dream.

Bisque turned around and then back to his grandmother, tilting—he whispered to her before kissing her on the ear and leaning his head against her chin, closing his eyes. His hand caressed her body.

"Mémère—I'll see you under the sun."

He put her on her back and covered her face with the blanket.

"Ç'est tout," he said, almost grinning like he knew a secret.

Back downstairs, Mr. Veron had fallen asleep in the kitchen area—his teeth on the table, he slumped in his chair with his mouth open, snoring. Bisque tapped him on the shoulder while he looked across the street—it was clear and gone, the house looked relieved after the fire had been put out. Bisque quietly called his name, then Mr. Veron lifted his head and without hesitation, he said—"Bread pudding."

"Yes," Bisque said. "Now it's time for some bread pudding."

Mr. Veron picked up his teeth and tapped them against the wood of the table.

"Should we bring it up to Violon?" he asked.

"Not today, Mr. Veron—she's asleep. She's in a good sleep."

Bisque took out two plates and spoons and started serving—the bread pudding still strong in its aroma. Before sitting down to eat, he went to the front of the church and opened the door, letting in the Gulf breeze, still tinted with the smell of smoke.

"Don't you worry, Mr. Veron," Bisque said. "You'll be good. I was thinking—you know Francis?"

"Sure do—that's Jeannette's son, right? He's the one who keeps on stealing from everyone, but then he returns it the very next day."

"That's him."

"That's a good kid."

"He's a good kid—I was thinking since your house is out right now, that you and Francis can help me put the farm back together and get it going again."

Mr. Veron put his teeth back in his mouth.

"Farm life," he said, smiling—"I miss it."

"Sounds good then," Bisque said.

He sat across from Mr. Veron and watched him take the first bite, and as soon as it entered his mouth, he made a sound—a sound of pure delight—and just before Bisque was about to take in his first spoonful, he noticed on his arm, scratches all along—as if he had been running through a pathway of branches—and coming from nowhere, he heard, as if from a long distance, the faint music of a familiar frottoir.

By the Pond Back Home

You MIGHT already know, but Turnip Redd's breakthrough performance came at the age of twenty-two on *Conan*. Shy, nervous, and overwhelmed, he was able to sing his "Let Me Be Gone" to a captivated audience, one that was completely silent after he finished. It wasn't until Conan himself started to clap when the rest of the audience gave Turnip a standing ovation.

"That was great," Conan said, shaking his hand. "Well done."

He patted Turnip on the back, as the singer slightly nodded while managing to smile.

"I'm a huge fan," Turnip said. "I saw a recording of when Elliott Smith played—"

The audience's cheer drowned out his voice as Conan led the show into credits. Turnip waved to the crowd—the studio lights had put him in a trance, and that was the beginning of it all.

That was ten years ago and after that show, his agent, Lester Danes, landed a deal with Sony Music, and Turnip became an instant success. The world was drawn to his soothing, innocent voice backed with his acoustic guitar, and with his low self-esteem and depressing lyrics, he formed a fan base ranging from teenagers to those who grew up in the 1960s. Incessant touring and interviews, endorsements ranging from whiskey to clothing lines to cars, Turnip grew up quickly in the entertainment world. No longer thin and frail—forty pounds heavier, a face scarred with sleepless nights of partying and fucking, all under the spell of alcohol and drugs—he wasn't the small-town boy from Youngsville, Louisiana, anymore.

Eight years after *Conan*, with red eyes and slurred speech, Turnip puffed on a cigarette and turned to Lester—they were in the greenroom, just before a show in Austin, Texas.

"You know—Lester—you know, I feel like this was what it was like in the '80s, you know. Like when Guns N' Roses and all, when they ruled the world. This must have been what it was like."

He blew the smoke out through his nostril.

"Not even, Ace," Lester said. "They have nothing on you. They wish they were you."

Lester sipped his drink and winked at his client. Turnip's demeanor changed—he watched the smoke twirl around in the air and thought about his wife and two children who were only six hours away, at home in Youngsville.

"Lester. Lester. Do you think Margaret knows what all that goes on? Like with all the women and the late nights and all?"

"Who cares, Ace. You've got to do whatever it takes to keep the show going. This is all you. This is you. It's you and no one else. What you're doing now—it gives them a home."

"Is this me?"

"Come on, Ace—sip up and smoke up. You're on in fifteen. I love you, pal."

"I love you, too."

Lester left the room, leaving Turnip alone with his thoughts, which he never wanted. He thought about his friend's burger spot in Youngsville and how he could be working there.

"That could still give us a home," he whispered and looked around the dim-lit room.

He dipped his hand into a bowl of M&M's, filtering out the colors, and popped a few red ones into his mouth. The lack of lighting in the greenroom was taking its toll on him, so he pulled out his phone and pressed 1.

"Hey Les, where'd you go?"

One cigarette was already lit, resting on the ashtray, but he lit a new one and took in a deep breath.

"Oh, okay. Yeah. I'm going to be out in a bit."

Turnip ran his hand through his hair and started pulling on it.

"Hey, Les—are you still there?"

He rubbed his eyes, not knowing if he was crying or if it was from the cigarette smoke.

"I miss the frogs, Les—you know what I mean? I miss hearing the frogs and listening to them croak at night just by the pond back home. I don't hear those frogs anymore, Les—I want to hear the frogs."

He kept the phone near his ear and listened to Lester, nodding his head up and down, gesturing, and saying "Okay, Les" when he got a chance. He hung up and there was complete silence—the silence Turnip dreaded. After popping another red M&M, he drank his whiskey in large gulps. After a coughing spasm, he threw his glass against the wall and stood up to get ready for his show. He took out a wrinkled photo of Margaret and his children—wallet size—of when they were at the park and feeding the ducks. After taking one more look at it, he crumpled it up and tossed it behind him.

"Fuck this."

That show in Austin marked the beginning of the end for Turnip, though some entertainment reporters who were documenting his growth argued that the end of Turnip had begun a long time ago, when his third album, *Far Too Dead*, was released, and he had completely left his life as a small-town musician and become fully caught up in the rock and roll world. Hospital trips, accidents—passing out during concerts and making a fool out of himself became his routine.

After he sang the last song of the night—a crowd favorite called "No More"—Turnip went back to the greenroom, where Lester had set up a post-show party. With a glitter ball twirling from the ceiling against a red light that shadowed the walls, the room was full of strangers, including those who backed him up onstage, and Turnip did what he knew best—he drank and smoked, conversed and joked around and fucked. One of his fans, who was invited by Lester, didn't necessarily want to party as the others did. She just wanted to talk about Turnip's songwriting and the meaning of some of his lyrics.

"Hey there," Turnip said in a shaky voice. "Would you like something to drink? What's your name? Are you from around here? Sorry, I'm kind of nervous and tired."

Turnip's head was looking for balance as it wavered left and right. He leaned back against the sofa—the red of the room matched the red of his eyes.

"I'm Caroline," she said.

"Sweet."

"I've been living here all my life, and I'm such a huge fan."

Turnip held up an empty glass, gesturing if she wanted a drink.

"No thanks. I'm actually four years sober today."

Turnip poured himself a glass. He felt comfortable being drowned out from all of the chattering and talking and laughing around him.

"That's amazing, Cassidy." He laughed. "Sorry, I meant Caroline."

Turnip offered her a cigarette, which she accepted. He lit hers and then his own and readjusted himself on the sofa.

"I just love your lyrics," she said. "I think about them all the time."

"You're kind. Thank you."

He waved to someone walking by.

"I just wanted to ask you about how you come up with such meaningful lyrics. They're so human, and I connect to them so much."

Turnip's head dropped over, and he nodded. Without looking up, he said, "Pain."

"Pain," Caroline said.

"All I have is pain."

"I understand."

He drank down his whiskey and poured another one while coughing. Turnip looked into Caroline's eyes—he wanted to kiss her and have sex with her for all its temporary purposes. He wanted to continue to escape from this world. His world.

Lester came over, handed Turnip a pill, and walked off without saying anything.

"This isn't a red M&M," Turnip said.

He laughed and swallowed the pill and washed it down with his whiskey.

"I guess I should leave," Caroline said. "It was so nice to meet you, and thank you for this invitation. It was such a great show."

Turnip remained silent.

"Bye," Caroline said.

She looked at him, waiting for a response, but Turnip was quiet—she got up, but just before leaving she tucked a piece of paper into his pocket. When Turnip awoke from his daze, he looked around for Caroline.

"Where'd you go?"

It wasn't too much later when his lips were on the neck of another—a member of the house band, hands and tongues everywhere. Turnip felt a tap on his shoulder.

"Ace."

He continued to kiss.

"Ace," Lester said again. "Your family is here."

He didn't hear his agent.

Lester laughed and patted Turnip on the shoulder.

"Have fun, Ace—you've earned it big time."

Drunk and stoned himself, Lester walked off. As he continued to kiss the bassist, Turnip recognized the scent of a perfume. He pulled his head back and rubbed his eyes.

"Your perfume," Turnip said. "I love it. It reminds me of home."

The bassist laughed.

"I'm not wearing any perfume. Maybe it's my lipstick."

Turnip messily shook his head.

"No. No. No. It's home. I know it. It's home."

He gulped his whiskey and poured another one—no matter how hard he tried to keep them open, his eyes were half closed, his head heavy.

Without saying a word, the bassist left, and Turnip felt a hand pressed under his chin, holding it up.

He grinned and breathed in.

"That perfume. That's home."

"Turny," Margaret said.

"Who's that? Is that you?"

Turnip only saw flashes of images before him, in rhythm with the twirling lights. He saw his wife's face. And for a moment, just before he leaned over and collapsed, he saw his two children's faces.

That became the last of Turnip Redd—as the world knew him. When Margaret picked Turnip up from the liquor-stained floor, the piece of paper Caroline had put in his pocket fell out. Margaret looked at it, thinking it was just another lady's phone number, but instead, it was a business card to a local addiction recovery center. Margaret received little help getting Turnip back on the sofa, and she looked around to see if anyone was in the right state of mind to help. Her children were trying their best not to cry, holding each other's hands and clinging to their mother's leg.

"Margaret," Lester said. "You made it."

"We need to get Turnip to the hospital."

"Oh he's not looking too good, is he? You missed a fantastic show—the crowd loved it. It was one of his best in a really long time. This should get him back on track, I think."

"Lester. You might want to clear this place out. I'm calling for an ambulance."

Lester hurriedly shouted for everyone to leave as Margaret was on the phone. As Turnip was taken into the ambulance, Caroline was still outside, talking with a few of her friends. She saw Turnip on the stretcher and ran over.

"Turnip, are you okay? Is he okay?"

"There's a pulse and he's breathing," Margaret said, tearing up. Her children were crying quietly behind her.

Caroline looked at her and the children. Turnip was being lifted up into the ambulance.

"You must be family."

"He's my husband," Margaret said.

She looked up into the sky.

"I think."

"I'm Caroline—I just talked to him like about an hour ago. I hope he'll be okay."

"Talk?"

Margaret held her children's hands as they tucked their heads into her legs.

"Oh. Talk. Yes, I promise. I just wanted to say hi. Please don't think—"

"No need to explain," she replied.

The ambulance pulled out of the parking lot.

"I need to go," Margaret said.

"If it's worth anything," Caroline said, "I put a card in his pocket."

"That was you?"

She nodded and smiled.

"Thank you."

"Take him straight from the hospital. It's the best way. Pack some clothes and all and bring it to the hospital, and then go from there."

"Hopefully. Thank you."

Caroline waved to the children, trying to help them feel a bit more at ease. The youngest waved back while the eldest remained shy.

As you might already know, Turnip Redd didn't die. After his stomach was pumped, he eventually became conscious again and spent three days in the hospital. Once awake, he called Margaret, but she didn't answer the phone or visit even though she was in the waiting room down the hall from his room. After speaking with the doctor, she and the children, who had spent the night in the hospital, got back into their truck and drove back home to Louisiana. Turnip, having no one else except for his agent, called Lester.

"I knew you'd be okay," Lester said.

Turnip fiddled with his blanket and the remote control.

"Did I make a fool out of myself again, Les?"

"Not at all, Ace. You're good—you're good. Everyone loves you."

"What's next?"

"I'll be there soon, Ace. I got to take care of some business, and I'll be there tomorrow."

"Sorry, Les."

"You're good, Ace. We'll get you back on tour in no time. Don't worry about it, Ace."

Turnip felt better after talking to Lester—he always did after he fucked up. The buzz from the ceiling lights made him sleepy. He flipped the channels on the TV, hoping not to find any reports on himself, and stopped on Nickelodeon—Turnip relied on sitcoms for comfort and watched an episode of *Friends*—the one where Chandler and Monica were trying to buy a house. After one more conversation with the nurse, Turnip called Margaret one more time—again, no response. He kept the TV on and went to sleep to the sound of laughter.

Margaret was exhausted. The back-and-forth trips from Youngsville to Austin and taking care of the children while worrying about the future of Turnip, their marriage, her job, had been taking its toll on her. She talked to Turnip once on the phone.

"I love you, Maggie."

"I'll see you tomorrow."

Turnip knew that he had fucked up too many times before, but this was the first time he had done so not only in front of Margaret but also with his children there.

"Will you bring the kids, Maggie?"

"I'll see you tomorrow."

As he waited for Margaret, he thought about their first date—on a humid summer night—it was Friday, and Turnip was sitting at the pond, looking up at the stars when he heard her voice.

"What are you wishing for," were the first words Margaret said.

The frogs were loud, and Turnip stuttered.

"You."

"Silly."

"I brought my guitar," Turnip said. "I wrote a song—do you want to hear it?"

"Silly."

That was the summer before their last year of high school—since then, they had been through it all.

Margaret's voice took Turnip out of his dream.

"Turnip."

"Turny?"

"I need your phone."

"Are the kids here?"

"We're about to get going—let me see your phone."

"I should call Les and let him know we're leaving."

"You can do that later."

Turnip handed Margaret his phone—the curtains were across the windows, and he asked Margaret to open them.

"Nothing more soothing than that natural light."

Margaret did as he asked, but that was it. She sat in silence while Turnip remained in bed, waiting to be released. He tried to talk to her, but she wasn't responding.

"I'm sorry," Turnip said. "I'm so sorry, Maggie. I've fucked up so much. I'm so sorry."

The nurse eventually came in with a wheelchair and he signed the papers. As they left the building, Margaret threw his phone away without Turnip noticing.

The car ride was quiet. Margaret drove the truck while Turnip looked at all the storefronts through the window. He knew not to say anything—he knew that she wasn't ready. Country music was playing quietly—Margaret's favorite kind—but neither of them were actually listening to it. He was shocked when they pulled into the parking lot of the addiction recovery center, which wasn't too far away from the hospital.

"What's going on, Maggie?"

She turned the volume down.

"Turny."

He felt better just by hearing her say that.

"If you want to save yourself, your relationship with your children, and your marriage—this is the first step."

"I can do this, Maggie, but I don't need to check in or anything. I can do it. You can help me."

"No. This is the first step, and I don't even know if it'll help, but it's the only start of anything that can maybe help."

Turnip shook his head and stuttered.

"Too many times," Margaret said.

She went on to talk about their children and what would happen if he died of an overdose or another accident or for whatever reason. They sat in the car for an hour—sometimes silent, sometimes talking. In that span of time, he craved a drink, a pill, a needle, anything that would help him not think anymore.

"Can I just get one more drink? Just a shot?"

Margaret teared up and shook her head.

"I miss the frogs, Maggie. I miss them."

"They're never going away—they're right there under the stars back home."

"By the pond."

"I packed a small bag of clothes and all. It's in the trunk."

"What about Lester?"

"What about him?"

Turnip understood. Margaret popped the trunk, and they both walked around the car.

"I love you," Turnip said.

Margaret opened her mouth and then paused—tears still coming down her face.

"You do."

A half-embrace, and Margaret watched Turnip walk to the entrance of the center. She watched him walk inside and got into the truck where she remained, there in the parking lot, for three hours, making sure that he didn't try to leave—making sure that he stayed. After those three hours, thinking that it was now safe, she went back home.

You probably didn't hear too much about Turnip while he was in rehab—other than that it was reported that he checked into one. He was there for 40 days: 40 days to change his whole life—to, if not overcome his addiction, to find ways to cope with it. Every night, after the day's activities were done, he'd call home, and Margaret would answer every time. Some nights were more conversational than others, and though it killed him, he didn't talk to his children. Even when he was on tour, he talked to his children more often, and he had never gone this long without hearing their voices.

"Everyone is nice here—they really want you to make it out ready, you know."

"That's good, Turny—and your voice sounds good. It's your voice—I hadn't heard you, like you, in so long."

"I like the lighting here, Maggie—it's always bright, and everything is just bright."

"That's good, Turny."

"When you come visit, Maggie, could you keep the kids at home? I don't want them to see me just yet."

"I wasn't going to bring them, but they miss you."

"Tell them I love them, Maggie. And I love you."

"I'll see you soon."

After their initial two weeks at the center, residents could have visitors on Saturdays. Turnip was nervous as he waited for Margaret to arrive. He had set a table and a couple of chairs in the corner of the dining area, trying to make it as intimate as possible. He had seen how the visits took place during the past two weekends, but it still didn't ease his anxiety. He made sure the coffee was fresh and that there was plenty of lemonade.

With his knees rocking up and down, and his hands tapping the tabletop, he watched as families entered, hugging the ones they were visiting. Then Margaret walked in, and Turnip stood up. He moved forward and then paused, looking at her, seeing what she was going to do—she hugged him. It was the hug that Turnip wanted when they were in the parking lot just a couple of weeks ago.

"Hey, we have a spot in the corner."

She followed him to their table.

"Would you like some coffee? Or some lemonade? The lemonade is really sweet here."

Margaret looked around the room as she sat down.

"You look great, Turny, you really do."

"I can't remember when my hair was this short," he said. "And when I had a shaved face, too."

"You've lost some weight."

"I've been exercising every day."

He laughed.

"Well I call it exercising. But basically a pound a day, give or take."

Margaret looked like she wanted to tear up. In the background, there was laughing and chatter, but it was all drowned out by Turnip's focus on his wife. They talked for the full two hours they were given—Turnip went to the courtyard a couple of times to smoke, but other than that they talked the whole time.

"They call me the thinker here, Maggie."

He laughed.

"Because all I do during my downtime is sit outside and stare at the garden."

"That's good, Turny."

"Are you proud of me, Maggie?"

"I am, Turny."

"I love you, Maggie. I really do."

"You do, Turny."

For the following weeks, both Turnip and Margaret became more comfortable with each visit. During the last visit—the following week, Turnip would go back home—Margaret brought Turnip drawings from their children.

"They're looking forward to seeing you," Margaret said.

"Are we good, Maggie?"

"What do you mean?"

"Are you going to split up with me, Maggie?"

"Let's just get you home first before we talk about anything else."

Turnip knew better than to ask, and he didn't mean to—it just came out.

"Have you heard from Lester? I thought he was going to come visit one day, or maybe even call."

Margaret's face hardened, but she remained patient. They hadn't talked about what Turnip would do once he returned until that Saturday. Would he still play music? Would he work at his friend's restaurant? Or maybe he would work at the auto shop—one of his favorite things to do was to work on cars.

"Let's be patient, Turny. There's no rush. We're good."

"One day at a time."

With that mantra in mind, Turnip had been clean and sober for two years now. He stayed away from the entertainment business or music or anything related to his previous life, focusing on family and health. The only time he picked up his guitar was to play for his children.

Lester? They had been in touch from time to time, but it was rare. A message here, a message there, but Turnip tried his best to stay away from anything that was connected to his previous life. They talked once on the phone, but overall, Lester wasn't too worried—after Turnip's initial success, the agent was able to acquire a solid list of clients, and he kept busy with them.

"Whenever you're ready, Ace," he said during the last time they spoke. "I'm here, pal."

That latest conversation took place just three weeks before Turnip played at his friend's burger joint. Turnip wasn't expecting to perform in public again—at least, not anytime soon—but it was Margaret who encouraged him after one night they were together at the pond. The sun was just coming down, and the two were having a picnic while the children were at their aunt's house.

"I got a song for you, Maggie."

"Let's hear it, darling."

Turnip lit a cigarette and strummed his guitar—Margaret was finishing her last bite of cold boudin. She closed her eyes and lay down in the grass. Turnip lifted his head toward the sky and hummed before he started singing his new set of lyrics, which was about Margaret and their children and fucking up so much in life but now having a second chance. He hummed out the ending of the song and strummed the strings one last time before finishing.

"What do you think, Maggie?"

"I think it's time."

Turnip lit another cigarette and puffed out the smoke with a loud breath.

"What do you mean?"

"You need to be out there, Turny. I think it's time. You're good. I know you're good. We're good. I'll be by you the whole time."

"You hear that?"

Margaret nodded.

"Those frogs, Maggie."

Three weeks later, Turnip found himself at his friend's restaurant—Chuckie's—in front of a small crowd of local fans, those who had been following Turnip since he was just a small-town teenager playing at various coffee shops and bars. He recognized every face, bringing him back to when he was just starting his career—faces he hadn't seen in years, since *Conan*.

"It has been awhile, y'all."

The fans cheered.

"Thank you all for coming out, and thank you to Chuckie for having me here."

He laughed.

"I'm nervous."

As he sat on a stool in a small open space in front of everyone, his knees rocked up and down. The crowd shouted again in support of Turnip.

"We missed you," Chuckie shouted from the kitchen.

Turnip looked around the room and saw Margaret and the children. The kids weren't too attentive as they were both investing their focus on the burgers, fries, and chocolate milkshakes. Turnip nodded at Margaret and pulled down his baseball cap, a ragged and torn faded blue hat, one that he had received as a gift while he was in high school from Margaret when they were first starting to date. Though Turnip had stopped wearing it for a long time, when his tours became larger and larger, Margaret kept it under his pillow for the nights, weeks, months he was away.

Turnip cleared his throat—craving a cigarette. He started to sing, lyrics first, and then he strummed his guitar. He sang the first tune he had ever performed live when he was a teenager at a lonely bar, one with only a few people, and they didn't give him any of their attention. It didn't take too long for the crowd to start singing along and mouthing the words to "Short Time Long." It was a six-minute song, and as Turnip looked around the room, he had visions from the past—anywhere from memories with Margaret, to his early shows, meeting Lester, his spot on *Conan*, through his peak days of singing and touring and fucking up. Flashes of all the wrong he had done—his addictions, the dark matter he kept in his mind at all times, the depressions and thoughts of suicide. As he worked on the last part of the song, the bright lights of rehab and holding hands with his children, fishing and cooking entered his thoughts. He closed his eyes and hummed out the ending. He opened his eyes and saw smiles, and cheering, and clapping. Margaret nodded her head—their children still focused on the milkshakes and coloring paper.

Turnip laughed.

"It has been awhile, y'all."

"Great to have you back," someone shouted from the audience.

"Thank you. Thank you."

Without hesitation, Turnip played his guitar and started singing again—he was going through his first ever set list from back when he was young. He went straight for an hour and a half, never taking a sip of water—the ridges of his hat slightly damp.

Turnip played more shows around Louisiana—New Orleans, Lafayette, Shreveport, and Baton Rouge. Margaret traveled with him as much as possible, by his side at all times to support him in both his music and sobriety, and when she couldn't make it, his sponsor from AA would go with him and do exactly the same. Turnip preferred to play at coffee shops and restaurants, but sometimes he sang in a few bars, and that was when he knew he must be aware of his surroundings as much as possible. He had only a few cravings for liquor and pills and anything else like that over the past two years or so, but for the most part, it wasn't anything too big for him to handle. However, he knew it would be best, at least for now, to always have support by his side when he played in these venues. During his downtime, he was able to make new songs, and he had a new set list.

"Would you ever believe it, Maggie? Twelve new songs?"

"I'm proud of you, Turny, in every way."

News had spread that Turnip was on the comeback. He left Louisiana sometimes, but not too far—Texas, Mississippi, Alabama, Georgia—just around the surrounding states. He had a small group of dedicated fans who followed him on tour. A music critic, J.M., who had given solid reviews of his prior albums and had been following his career with frequent interviews, had gone to one of his new shows when he had heard that Turnip was playing again. This time around, Turnip's songs weren't received well by J.M., who wrote that there were remnants of Turnip's brilliance, but the depth and the emotion-evoking lyrics from his previous years were no longer apparent. "There is pain and sorrow in these lyrics and in his voice," J.M. wrote, "but the darkness is no longer there." He ended his article congratulating Turnip on his sobriety, while also hoping for mirrors of his previous songs. "That," J.M. wrote, "would be the ultimate comeback."

Turnip grinned as he read the review of one of his recent shows. He was in Baton Rouge, on his way back home from a tour, giving one last show before returning to Margaret and the children. It was a three-week tour, and though Turnip was still facing anxiety while playing, especially because he couldn't mask away any of his emotions through whiskey and pills, he learned to cope with it and play. Facing his fans, not being numb with distorted realities, he no longer felt alone and isolated. He felt a longing to be heard.

"That J.M. came down hard on me, Jay."

His sponsor patted him on the shoulder.

"Good."

He winked.

"It's about that time—are you ready?"

Turnip puffed the last out of his cigarette and put it out. He looked at some of the previous concert bills hanging on the walls of the greenroom and focused on the one for Elliott Smith when he was touring for *XO*.

"Never."

He smiled.

Just as he was about to get up, there was a knock on the door. Jay looked at Turnip, and he nodded, but before his sponsor was able to open the door, the handle turned, and Lester walked in.

"What do you say, Ace?" Lester said.

Turnip remained on the couch and lit another cigarette.

"Hey there."

Lester shook Jay's hand and introduced himself.

"I'm Ace's agent."

Jay just nodded his head, not saying anything else.

"It's okay, Jay—could you give us a second?"

"Sure thing. I'll be right outside."

Turnip knew that it would happen at some point—meeting Lester again—but he wasn't expecting it that particular night. He felt his heart beat fast, an emptiness in his stomach.

"Okay? What do you mean it's okay, Ace? I'm your pal, Ace—your agent. We've been through it all, Ace."

Just hearing himself being called that name made Turnip shudder.

"It's nothing, Lester."

He exhaled smoke.

"And please—let's just go with Turnip."

Lester sat down next to him.

"I missed you, Ace—Turnip. I really did."

"I've just been doing my thing."

"It hurt hearing that you've been playing and touring without letting me know—with a new set of songs, too."

"It's nothing big—just having a bit of fun. It feels nice. It feels real good."

"I saw a recording of you playing in Athens not too long ago."

Lester looked at the magazine sitting on the coffee table.

"I read it," he said. "Not good."

"I don't mind it."

Lester stood up and started pacing back and forth—one hand on his forehead, the other on his hip.

"We got to get you back, Ace."

Turnip lit another cigarette and took a sip of his coffee. Jay opened the door and peered in.

"You good, Turnip?"

"All good—I'll be out in a bit."

Lester sat back down.

"Do you realize how big you can be? Going through rehab, making a comeback, you can be huge. Much bigger than before, Ace."

"It's just not my thing anymore. I like playing these shows."

"But he's right," Lester said.

He tapped his fingers on the magazine.

"You've got to get that voice back—those words back—the pain back. This can get you back on track—think about the album sales, the awards, the concerts. It'll be like nothing you've seen before, Ace."

"I'll be okay," Turnip said. "I got pain, I got regret, I got remorse, I got sadness. But I have something that I didn't feel before—for a long time. I have love. I feel happy."

"Love? Happy? Ace—listen to yourself, that's not you. We need the old Ace back."

"Turnip."

"Listen, Ace—think how you can set your family, your children, for the rest of their lives."

Turnip thought about fishing back home with his children.

"We'll be okay."

Lester walked to the door, locked it, and sat back down.

"Let's do this, Ace."

He pulled out a flask and a prescription bottle and put it on the coffee table.

"What do you say, Ace? Let's get you back. We need you. This will get you where you need to be."

Turnip stared at the flask and the bottle of pills. He exhaled smoke, watched it travel around in circles and waves, and felt the emptiness in his stomach. Just as he was about to speak, Lester's phone rang.

"Hold on."

He stood up and answered the call. Turnip looked at the coffee table again. He checked his own phone and saw that he had a voicemail from Margaret. He looked at the flask and the bottle of pills and thought about his previous life. He looked at Lester, who was gesturing and talking in a loud voice—Turnip observed his face, a face he no longer recognized, one that was cracked and bruised and torn. His eyes—hollow. He listened to Margaret's message and grinned.

"I love you, Turny."

That was all he needed to hear. By the time Lester had finished his conversation, Turnip had left the room—getting ready for his first song of the set list. His agent turned around and didn't see him. He opened the door and looked down the hallway and saw nothing.

"Damn it, Ace."

And if you were there—there somewhere in the hallway, you could faintly hear Turnip introducing himself while strumming the guitar. "Here's my first song of the night," he said. "It's a new one."

You could hear the crowd shouting and clapping, and then when the audience quieted down, you could hear him say the name of his latest song. Another roar, another loud applause—and there, way in the back, in the shadows of the hall, you could see Conan sitting there, wearing a cowboy hat and a faded khaki jacket—Turnip strummed his guitar and started to sing.

Atchafalaya Darling

WHEN THE WIND came in, so came in the memories of Belle—much like the chimes on Arcade's front porch during those summer night breezes amid mosquitoes and the buzzing cicadas, there were echoes of his daughter's voice in swirling air. Vague in muffled sounds of shifting limbs and branches and breaking currents, as one bright pelican, solo and meditative, swooped down for a grasp and pulled away forever into the sky with a victorious beak, Arcade closed his eyes and let his ears feel the pressures of the world. Just next to him, on the deck of the houseboat that he and Belle had built themselves, was an ice chest filled with chilled Ruston peaches—his daughter's favorite fruit.

The houseboat was still half broken, wrecked from a storm three years before—the same day he had lost his daughter. The back portion had caved in, the bunk beds had tilted over—a broken microwave, a detached and cracked stovetop—there was clutter everywhere, remnants of the worst day of Arcade's life. The front deck was still intact, but it needed reinforcements where some of the wood had split. He hadn't been back since the storm, and as he was sitting on the porch of his house—the chimes, it was something about the chimes swaying and sounding that made him return to his home on the water.

He sifted his hair with his hands and looked at the cypress trees, some still bent and broken from the storm, and he thought about how he and Belle had built the houseboat over a span of a year. She was fourteen then, eager to help her dad. He loved how she would stick her tongue out and squint when hammering away on boards or how she would gulp down a bottle of Mountain Dew and smile right after, saying, "Fresh rain."

"Your mom would be proud of you," Arcade said, after one full day of work on the boat.

"She'd be so mad at me," Belle said, laughing. "Barefoot with all these nails around?"

"Oh she would have been mad at me instead," Arcade said. "She'd be proud of you."

"Daddy, tell me again how she left."

"Oh the river took her, darling. And that's why it looks so beautiful out here."

Belle patted her dad on the shoulder.

"Every time I see a blue heron, I think about her."

Since the storm, Arcade had difficulty in differentiating the voices of Belle and her mother. When he recalled memories, day by day, the sound of their voices combined into one as if their deaths were tributaries into the Mississippi. Just next to the ice chest were eight large cinder blocks. He gently kicked one to see if it would nudge and pulled out a can of dip and quietly laughed when he thought about Belle putting some in her mouth for the first time.

"You sure got sick didn't you, darling?"

Arcade felt the burn and spat out in the water. There was still light, and the wind kept talking to him. Just as he was about to walk inside he heard a voice coming from the water.

"Belle?"

The voice became louder.

"Is that you, darling?"

He could see a body bobbing in the Atchafalaya.

"Is that you, Belle?" he called out.

Arcade pulled out a fishing rod from inside—unscathed from the storm—and started to wave it back and forth, finding a rhythm before releasing the line.

"Go on and grab it," Arcade shouted.

The body was coming closer—the voice was still hard to hear in the wind. Arcade reeled back and threw the line again. This time, he felt a pull.

"Come on now," he whispered.

He squinted.

"Don't tug on it," he shouted. "Just hold on to it—let it guide you."

He could clearly see the figure.

"That's not you," Arcade said.

He knew it wasn't her, but there was always a bit of hope—the kind of hope that eases sorrow just for a tease. Arcade saw a man with a big grin on his face—one missing tooth right in the front. The man waved.

"What are you doing out here like that?" Arcade said.

"My canoe fell over."

He waded in the water and turned his head to look behind.

"I lost my oar."

Arcade looked at the cinder blocks again and then the ice chest. He spat—overhead, as the wind shuffled about, there was a crane flying, its wings blanketing the sky. Arcade didn't want any company, but there was nothing else he could do other than to just let him float away. He watched the crane disappear in the shine of the sun.

"Come on over, and I'll pull you up."

The man swam up to the edge of the deck. He waved again.

"I'm Bartholomew."

Arcade bent over and stuck his hand out, grunting as Bartholomew clumsily pulled himself over with his help. He lay flat on his back, breathing hard. The sun was just starting to come down.

"Damn," Bartholomew said, still huffing. "I think it's going to rain."

Arcade looked around, lifting his head.

"Maybe so. You okay?"

His loud breathing evened out, and he sat himself up with arms crossed over his knees.

"Damn."

"I might have a dry shirt, maybe some shorts. Hold on a second."

He went into the cabin and pushed aside the clutter, going back to the bunk beds, pushing a mattress over. There was a bag—Belle's bag. Arcade took a deep breath and opened it, trying to push away the memories for the moment. There was a vague familiar scent. Arcade thought that the man was skinny enough to wear her yellow shirt and green shorts.

"Always helping out aren't you, darling?"

He pictured her wearing those clothes while working on the houseboat—looking bright and energetic under the sun. He zipped the bag closed and carefully put it aside, against the wall.

"It might not be a perfect fit."

Bartholomew thanked him as he peeled off his soaked shirt. Arcade looked out into the basin as the stranger put on the green shorts, which came up to his upper thighs.

"I like the colors," he said, thanking Arcade again. "It reminds me of sunshine, you know. Damn."

"You lost your tooth out there?" Arcade asked.

Bartholomew moved his tongue to feel the gap.

"I don't think so," he said.

"What happened to it?"

"To what?"

"Your tooth."

"I was young then, I think—I can't quite remember."

"Strange."

Bartholomew looked at the ice chest.

"I'm too much of a bother," he said. "But do you have a beer I could use?"

"I don't."

Arcade saw him looking at the ice chest.

"I have a Capri Sun."

"Capri Sun—wow."

"You can have one," Arcade said.

Bartholomew bent down to open the ice chest.

"Hold on," Arcade said quickly. "Let me get it for you."

"You have your family with you here? You know, Capri Sun—I was just thinking."

Arcade opened the ice chest and carefully shifted a few pears around—he pulled out a Capri Sun and gave it to Bartholomew.

"Something like that," Arcade said.

He pulled out a pear and wiped it off.

"Always helping someone out aren't you, darling," he whispered to himself.

"What's that?" Bartholomew asked.

"Here."

Bartholomew took one big bite into the fruit—a loud crunch.

"I don't have much else," Arcade said. "Just pears and juice."

"That's plenty."

Evening had settled in—the sun cut in half—and so entered the songs of the frogs and the buzz of insects. The wind kept coming, taking with it a call from an owl perched not too far away.

"You can sleep here for the night," Arcade said. "And tomorrow, when the sun comes, we can take the motorboat and take you back to the dock to get you back on land."

Bartholomew thanked him as he munched away on a second pear. Arcade brought out two mosquito lanterns and hung them up on the cabin.

"My family will be worried," Bartholomew said. "But there's really nothing we can do."

"I'd give you my phone, but I don't have one."

Arcade took out a pear and gently pushed on its skin, almost like he was petting it.

"You have a family," Arcade said.

"My wife Coraline and two daughters, Lydiane and Violette."

He paused.

"I love them."

"Sure thing," Arcade said.

He put the pear in his pocket and took out his dip, tapping it against his thigh.

"You want some?" Arcade said.

He took a pinch and tucked it in against his gums then handed the can to Bartholomew. He did the same.

"You have a family?" Bartholomew asked.

"I do."

"They're at home?"

"Something like that," Arcade said. "I should see them soon."

The air was humid—their skin, damp, as they sat at the table on the deck. Bartholomew looked around as Arcade was setting his fishing rod again.

"This place looks pretty hurt," Bartholomew said.

"It needs some work," Arcade said. "The big storm had its way—lost a lot."

Bartholomew was talking, but Arcade didn't hear him. He was taken back into a memory as he listened to the owl. The wind pushed through his skin, his eyes closed as bright Polaroid flashes of the past simmered in his head. How it went—the way Belle floated in his mind in gleam like an antique photo covered in sunspots, all so shiny to where Arcade leaned forward to grasp a better view as if she was right in front of him. There, in the front yard of their home, the green grass so bright and bold, a shimmer, as Belle was on her knees holding scissors. The light tinkering and playing with his vision—somewhere he could still hear the owl's calling, not letting him completely depart and venture into the past.

The chimes were there—a magic trick in itself—and so was Aubin, sitting in a rocking chair next to Arcade. The following year she would be gone, and up until that day, she was the one who kept the family together, the spirit of the household. Never was she seen as mad or impatient or unkind, and it was her teeth that Arcade missed the most, when she smiled under a large pair of sunglasses while they were drinking homemade lemonade on the porch watching the sun descend. As it flickered, Arcade saw Belle—in and out—as she cut carrot flowers in bunches, and just at the edge of the yard, a broken lawn mower. She was singing—Arcade heard it—switching back and forth between "This Little Light Of Mine" and "Jambalaya," over and over like they were made to be sung together.

"Daddy."

"Yes," Arcade said out loud, reaching out his hand.

The owl was still there, pocketed in the wind.

"Daddy, the sun looks so sad when it comes down like that."

"Never sad, darling—just sleepy, that's when the moon appears."

"Do you think the sun and the moon are friends?"

Arcade with his hand still out—his index finger stretched, pointing to his memory.

"Sure thing, darling. They can never be separated."

Aubin was mute—she rocked in her chair, its creaking in unison with the twirl of the porch fan.

"How about some pancakes tonight?" Arcade said, rocking in his own chair, in rhythm. "My own very special homemade pancakes and blueberries out from the back—just for my two darlings."

Aubin spoke, her smile in full form, but Arcade couldn't make out what she was saying.

"What's that, darling?" he said, as the wind shook the basin.

He could hear the chimes. Her voice faded away.

"Daddy," Belle said again.

She held a bunch of carrot flowers in her hands, some in her hair.

"Where does the wind go?"

As Arcade was about to answer, he heard shuffling—it was near. It was familiar. The owl's song, hidden—the chimes in his head, gone. Arcade shook his head.

"Sir," he said.

He spat.

"Sir."

Bartholomew, who was bent over the ice chest, his arm rustling the ice, stood up.

"Yes, sir," he said.

"What do you need?" Arcade said.

"I was just looking to see if there was anything else. I'm sorry."

"You won't find much else there—just juice and pears."

"I'm just seeing that I don't know your name," Bartholomew said.

"That's right," he replied. "It's Arcade."

Arcade looked at the ice chest and took a deep breath.

"Look," he said.

He stuck his hand in the chest and pushed the ice around, digging all the way to the bottom, and pulled out a music box. It was cherry red with a bronze lining.

"This is my daughter's," Arcade said.

"It's pretty."

He paused for a second.

"How come it's in an ice chest?"

"I just figured it'd be safe. She loved pears and juice, so I just thought I'd keep it there."

"Maybe funny," Bartholomew said.

Arcade rubbed the music box with his palms, humming to himself. Bartholomew sipped on another Capri Sun while eating another pear—his fourth one.

"I'm sorry for taking all of your food and drink."

Arcade continued to hum, staring into the water—the houseboat rocked in the wind, the ropes tied around four wooden posts, pushing and pulling, making the boat sound like it was hungry. Bartholomew called out Arcade's name a few times before he ventured out of his daze—it wasn't the stranger's voice that brought him back, but he had opened the music box, not realizing that he was doing so, and the melodies of a harp woke him up.

Inside was a charm necklace, which was catching the light from the mosquito lantern.

"It's my daughter's," Arcade said.

"It's pretty and shiny," Bartholomew said.

"She sure is," he replied.

The wind became stronger.

"I guess it's coming," Arcade said. "Let's bunk up inside and see how it looks in the morning."

Bartholomew followed him inside the cabin and helped him clear up some space. Arcade put down a blanket.

"It won't take me long to sleep," Bartholomew said. "Dead tired—thank you for being so kind. I know this isn't how you probably wanted to enjoy the day out here."

"It's fine—everything is going to be okay."

He took out his can of dip and put another pinch against his gums.

"I'll see you in the morning."

Bartholomew didn't lie—it didn't take more than five minutes for him to sleep. Arcade went back outside and sat at the table. The music box was still open, and he fiddled with the charm necklace, twisting around between his fingers, undoing it, and then twisting it again. It was just the wind and the voices in his head that kept him company.

"I'll see you soon, darling," he said.

Just as he spoke, it started to drizzle. In the distance, Arcade could see lightning flashes, and he heard the air rumble.

"Fresh lightning," he said.

He held up Belle's charm necklace—as it flickered in the strikes from the sky, so did his memories. The drizzle turned into rain, and Arcade knew that it was time—it was his signal. He threw the locket into the air and let the wind take it, as if he was releasing ashes from an urn into the ocean, an urn he was never able to hold—his daughter's body, never turned into ashes or buried or found.

The houseboat rocked in the turbulent water—Arcade looked through the sliding door of the cabin, and he saw that Bartholomew was still sleeping.

"Strange," he said. "Stranger."

The rain came down, and Arcade could only see what was right before him—he went to the side of the houseboat and dragged pieces of rope from around the corner. The thunder was louder, the lightning near.

"Come," Arcade said.

He took one more pinch of dip and put the can on the table, leaving it for Bartholomew. The basin was loud—muting all other sounds of life. Arcade ran the rope through each of the eight cinder blocks, his hands burning from the friction. He struggled as the boat wavered—the ropes heavier in the rain. He spat. The mosquito lanterns no longer in glow, he waited for the lightning to gain his bearings—letting that brief flash guide him in his tasks. One by one, he was able to fasten the rope through each block.

"Perfect," he said.

That day—three years ago, Belle and Arcade were relaxing on the houseboat. It was June—they were there to celebrate Aubin's birthday. The weather turned so quickly—Arcade didn't think that it was going to be big, just another thunderstorm with wind and lightning and sporadic heavy downpours. It came during their second night on the boat, after two full days of fishing and grilling, talking—and Belle would read out loud to Arcade, who never really liked books, but he loved to listen to his daughter read. Since Aubin's death, Belle was the only one who could make Arcade laugh, too. The weather was pretty during those two days, and when the wind picked up and the evening clouds darkened, they stayed in the cabin as the houseboat rocked with no control in the water. The air flashed blue through the window as they counted seconds between silence and thunder. The rain came down hard and fast. Arcade kept Belle unworried by telling her stories of when he was a boy and all of his mischievous antics, which included stealing a tractor in the dark and running it into a ditch while trying to get away from its owner.

"Why'd you steal it, Daddy?"

"It looked like a rhinoceros, and I was pretending that we were friends—riding away across the fields."

"That didn't last too long."

"No more than five minutes, darling."

"Did you get in trouble?"

"It wasn't looking too good, between the owner and your grandfather, but they couldn't stop laughing at me. I had to work on the farm to help pay off the damages."

Belle was chewing sunflower seeds, and she spat them in a milk carton just as Arcade would spit his tobacco into a can. They talked well into the night—two hours of stories and laughing—and it became the best night Arcade ever had with his daughter.

As the houseboat rocked in the water, they heard a large cracking sound, which caused the houseboat to shake even more in the storm.

"Hold up, darling," Arcade said. "You stay here—stay sat, and I'll be right back."

Arcade could tell by the look on Belle's face that she didn't want him to go out on the deck.

"I'm going with you, Daddy."

"Darling, please just stay sat—I'll be right back, I promise."

He grabbed a flashlight. The thunder came, frightening both Arcade and Belle, as they lowered their heads and lifted their shoulders.

"Oh that's just my stomach, darling," Arcade said. "I'm really hungry."

Belle smiled, and he walked out onto the deck. After his first step, he knew he had made a bad decision—there was nothing to see. The rain and the dark swirled around him—dizzying any kind of vision. The flashlight didn't spread much, but Arcade knew his houseboat well enough to walk on the deck toward one of the corners, where the boat was tied to a post. He held onto the table as he guided himself out to the edge and knelt. With the rain pelting and stinging the back of his neck and head, Arcade shone the flashlight and saw that the post had broken and the rope was loose. He tugged on it and pulled it up over the edge to tie it again over the broken post—the part that was still lodged into the basin bed. An embrace.

"Darling," Arcade said. "It's dangerous."

Belle didn't let go, pressing her face against his back.

"Darling," Arcade said. "Please."

And the lightning struck, and the cypress fell—leaning over the roof of the houseboat, and when Belle turned around, its limbs struck her in the head, breaking off from the trunk and taking her with its own sorrow into the Atchafalaya. Arcade felt her embrace let go—a glow behind him, a tree on fire—he looked around and called her name. Just next to him—her charm necklace, shining and reflecting the rain—and he grabbed it while shouting her name into the thunder. He pulled the rope up again, hands shaking, and tied it around his waist, jumping into the basin.

In the darkness, he grabbed nothing—nothing to be seen, he stayed under, and went down as far as he could go, and he came back to the surface, swimming and grasping nothing, and back he dove again in search of Belle. The rain was loud as it hit the water—Arcade gave no heed to the dangers of the storm—relentless in his desperate plea with the sky, he didn't stop. The storm calmed—early morning, the remains of disaster, quiet and wounded, Arcade, with the rope still around his waist, floated on his back, his eyes full of loss. He gathered strength and made his way back to the houseboat, grunting as he pulled himself over with the help of the broken post. A burnt cypress and toppled trees— Arcade put his hand in his pocket and pulled out Belle's necklace, and the crying began.

"I'll be there, darling," Arcade said.

He held on to the table as he secured the rope around his waist, and one by one, he moved each cinder block to the edge of the deck. Looking up, he let the rain hit his face, cold and hard, sticking out his tongue. He couldn't tell if he was crying—the rumbling thunder echoed in his head, a lightning strike, and Arcade picked up a cinder block, grunting and heaving, lifting it above his head. He felt an embrace around his waist.

"Darling."

"Hold on," Bartholomew said.

"Belle."

"Hold on."

He pulled Arcade back, both tumbling over each other, a corner of one of the blocks cutting Arcade's forehead. The blood came.

"I got you," Bartholomew said, over and over.

"Who are you?"

"Hold on."

"Let me go."

A thunder—a lightning flash—a strong gust of wind, and the house-boat shook, almost like it was anxious. As Bartholomew tried to stand up while also pulling up Arcade, he hit the ice chest and it toppled over—pears and juice slid across the deck. Bartholomew picked up one of each and tucked them into his shorts. He saw the music box—the harp faintly playing along with the rain—and shut it closed before gently sliding it toward the cabin door. Arcade tried to run to the edge of the deck, but Bartholomew held onto his hand, not letting him get away.

"I got you," Bartholomew said.

"Let me go."

"I can't."

"I'm going to see my daughter."

"Where?"

"She's there somewhere. Let me go."

"I can't."

As the storm calmed—the sky quieting, and the thunder now sounding like a distant machine whirring its last breath—Arcade cried. It was a loud cry, his voice hoarse and broken, and he put his head down and let the tears of three years fall from his face. Bartholomew pulled him in and hugged him, Arcade's face buried into his chest as he cried. He remained silent—the stranger—and let Arcade cry until his chest slowed down. He pulled away but still held Arcade's hand.

"Let's get this off of you."

Arcade didn't speak, staring at the edge of the deck, and as the last of the fire gave out, so did the vision of the deck's horizon, darkness. Bartholomew struggled to untie the rope, but he was able to get it loose—

it plopped onto the wood. Before doing anything else, he made sure to throw each cinder block into the basin. Arcade was quiet as he watched Bartholomew work. In the dark, the yellow shirt and green shorts became apparent, almost glowing. Arcade sat down cross-legged and the stranger—the man who kept him from dying—lay on his back, waiting for his breath to slow down.

"I got a pear and a Capri Sun," Bartholomew said. "It looks like the rest of them are all done."

The wildlife started to breathe again—birdsongs as the houseboat slowly creaked in the calm waters.

"You want it?" Bartholomew asked.

Arcade peered around the cabin and saw that the motorboat was still attached.

"I'm good," he said.

He reached over and picked up the can of dip, which hadn't fallen too far away from the table, and put in a pinch, his eyes sore from crying. And the sun rose as the humidity settled in—a pink and orange glow coming from beyond. They sat there on the deck, quiet, and watched the morning come, and as the sun made its way, Arcade finally spoke.

"We'll take the motorboat and head on over to the landing. Your family must be worried about you."

"It's pleasant," Bartholomew said.

"Thank you."

Bartholomew's eyes became large and pointed.

"Oh look," he said. "There's another Capri Sun."

He laughed.

"You want it?"

"You take it."

Arcade stood and looked around, but it was all a haze to him. He listened and focused on the chirp of a cardinal—in rhythm, it sang after short pauses. In the water, he saw a turtle wading through as if nothing had happened—no storm, just another morning.

"Let's get going," he said.

He revved the engine and the motorboat took off—Arcade in the back with the music box and Bartholomew in the front. They headed toward the sun, sitting quietly—there was no need to talk, but if Arcade turned around, back at the houseboat, he would see that there was sparkle coming from the burnt cypress where Belle's charm necklace swayed softly on a leaning branch.

A Vermilion Sad Song

A RECKONING—WHEN BALE Distefano played the fiddle—furious in movement, violent hands and maddened strings, her face so in focus that her eyes seemed to wander off into the air amid the melodies of her own instrument. Such precision—her gritted teeth and staunch neck, the way her lips remained motionless while she herself caused such movement, dizzying her audience until the world became mute.

Even the Vermilion could glitter some days under a kind sun in the morning. Bale sat on its bank, just under the bridge. The humidity hadn't settled in yet, and the call of the owl could be heard from afar, drifting in and out between the wind and the traffic above. She was surrounded by litter—shoes, bottles, cans, paper bags, plastic bags, Popeyes—the clutter didn't bother her unless the trash was in her favorite spot, between two large shrubs that helped to shield her from the heat with a bit of shade. She saw the glimmer of the Vermilion, focusing on a piece of wood floating with the current. The river was bloated that morning, still healing from a week's rain, causing flooding throughout Lafayette. Some homes and businesses were just recovering from the previous hurricane season, and they had to start all over again after record-high rains.

"Cut," Bale said.

Bale herself was also healing after not making the cut for a spot in the local band, Fricassee, a group of musicians who were making the scene by opening for the Lost Bayou Ramblers.

Again—"Cut," she said.

It wasn't so much that Bale didn't get the spot that bothered her, though of course it did hurt a bit, but it was more so who became the fiddler for Fricassee that troubled her. Ami. Ami was the fiddler—a former boyfriend, a bad split. They were together three years ago, meeting at The Bizarre for an open mic event—it was Ami's first live performance, while Bale had been a regular for the weekly series.

"I haven't seen you around," Bale said.

Ami stuttered after taking a sip of his drink.

"It's my first time here."

Bale saw his fiddle case leaning against his leg.

"I play the fiddle, too."

"I just started playing about a year ago—you?"

"Since I was five or so—my Pa and Ma were fiddlers. It's in the genes I guess."

"My dad played, too—you know The Cajun Coo?"

Bale nodded while looking around the room, studying the crowd.

"He used to play for them."

"I've seen them a million times—I know who you're talking about. He's amazing."

"Thanks."

He looked around the room as well.

"Is the lineup set yet?" Bale asked.

She glanced at the wall where it usually hung on a beaten-up clipboard.

"I'm fourth," Ami said.

Bale walked up to the list and counted.

"Eighth."

Bale could tell that Ami was nervous, and though she wanted to talk to some of her friends and the regulars at the venue, she stayed with Ami so that he wouldn't focus too much on his upcoming performance. She thought he was handsome and polite, sure, but that was all. It wasn't until he got up onstage and started playing when she became attracted to him—the way he pursed his lips, tightened his forehead, and moved his body as he played.

Once he was playing, he didn't look nervous to Bale, but in a place where he was supposed to be. They didn't get a chance to talk after—he was surrounded by people wanting to congratulate him, and Bale didn't want to be a bother. She sat and waited for her turn, occasionally looking at Ami, perhaps to get his attention, but he was far too immersed in his conversations and drinks and having a good time. Bale finally got his attention when she went up to perform. Tapping her feet and sounding a rooster's call before she played her fiddle, it was the one time she looked into the audience while playing, as usually she stared at the floor before her or up toward the ceiling, but never at the crowd. She caught his eyes and fell in love in the middle of the song, "The Morning Rise," one of the few songs she had put lyrics to—about farm life and its morning chores. Singing in Cajun French and English, she bellowed as she had never done before, feeling her throat travel down to her stomach. Tears came down her face—all of her strength revealed through her song.

"Thank you," she said, breathing hard.

The audience applauded and cheered her on, making Bale smile. Her plaid shirt was drenched in sweat. Ami approached her as she walked off the stage and hugged her as if they had been friends for years. Bale looked at his teeth.

"Mesmerizing," he said. "I was taken away."

Normally not shy, Bale didn't know how to respond—she patted him on the shoulder and tilted her head forward, feeling grateful. As they played more shows at the same venues, whether it was at The Bizarre or elsewhere, Bale and Ami became close friends, and at times, they performed as a duo. Their first kiss—after a show, outside on a humid night, both holding their fiddles—Bale knew that she was in trouble because it was the first time she'd felt this way about someone. She didn't want to be in a relationship, only wanting to focus on her career, seeing if there was a way to make a living out of it while bussing tables at Randol's Seafood Restaurant.

They moved into an apartment together on University Avenue—split the bills, shared groceries, washed each other's laundry, had sex, drank together, listened to music—Bale had become more and more comfort-able with Ami. Her family was welcoming, and the same with Ami's, and Bale soaked in as much as she could from Ami's dad, Amiot, in awe of his talent and experience.

Bale watched a turtle wade in the Vermilion as she thought about her time with Ami.

"Cut," she said.

Those memories darkened as their breakup entered her mind. The gist of it? Ami loved someone else, and it wasn't so much that he loved someone else that troubled Bale, but the pain came when she found out that they were affectionate with each other while she and Ami were still together—this was through a mutual friend who was also a musician. It was how it happened that Bale couldn't forgive, espe-cially as it was Bale's first relationship, one where she gave it her all to someone else and opened herself up—a way of life she wasn't used to before meeting Ami.

"I'm sorry, Baley," Ami said.

They were on the balcony of their apartment.

"Don't call me that," Bale said. "No more."

"What do you want me to say? Don't be jealous."

This had set Bale off to the point where she eventually couldn't even speak anymore. There were no tears, just anger, and remaining silent, she packed her belongings and drove thirty minutes home to her parents' house. It was there where she let her tears out, crying on her mother's shoulder while her dad rubbed her back in consolation.

What made it worse was that Bale knew the other lady—the one Ami left her for, Fabienne—long before she met Ami. They had gone to junior high together, and Fabienne being the only Black student in the class, standing out from the rest of her classmates just by the color of her skin and her hair and her family, Bale defended her whenever she was being teased. She helped her with her classwork, too, and they eventually became close friends until they parted ways for high school. Fabienne was a musician herself—the lead singer and guitarist for a local indie band called The Roux Roux Dolls who were well established by the time both Bale and Ami were emerging artists in the Lafayette circuit. Much like during junior high, Fabienne was the only Black singer among the indie pop bands in the city—her ripping voice and stage presence had immediately attracted the crowds, and it didn't take too long for The Roux Roux Dolls to sign with a local record label, SoleilSoleil.

Bale couldn't help but think that it was Fabienne's connection with SoleilSoleil that led Ami to leave her in hopes of moving his career forward with his music, especially getting into playing the fiddle in non-traditional styles, such as with rock or pop music—something that Bale would never imagine doing. Bale had admired Fabienne, though, and they would watch each other play and casually tell each other hi, but that was the extent of it.

Was it her eyes, Bale thought—the back of her neck burning as the sun rose. Her pretty eyes—her body or her voice? All of those qualities of Fabienne's came to mind as she wondered why Ami left her for Fabienne.

"Cut," she said.

She fiddled with the patches of grass around her, trying to get comfortable as the day became hotter. Even as it glittered, the Vermilion looked sad to Bale, and she held her breath, attempting to listen to its current—to hear if the river had words for her.

When Bale heard about the opening for Fricassee, she was excited—hopeful and confident about joining them. She knew the members of the group, and they had been cordial and welcoming. She restrung her dad's fiddle and used his instead of her own for good luck, and put on her favorite shoes, which she seldom wore. The audition was held at one of the band member's houses, which Bale had visited before for random parties and small shows. When she arrived, her mood changed as she saw Ami and Fabienne sitting on the stoop of the house. Ami was smoking a cigarette, which surprised Bale because he wasn't a smoker when they were together.

"Fuckhead," she mouthed, while trying not to look at them.

Both Ami and Fabienne stood up. Bale, knowing that there was no way of avoiding them, continued to walk straight, feeling the emptiness in her stomach.

"Hey, Bale," Ami said.

Fabienne waved.

Bale walked straight through, going between them without saying a word.

"Oh come on, Bale," Ami said.

"Let her be," Fabienne said.

She stood at the front of the door with her back to them and knocked on the door. It felt like the longest ten seconds to Bale, but eventually the door opened.

"Hey, Roman."

Roman was her favorite of all the members—kind and considerate, no ego. She walked in, and they went to the living room where all the equipment was set up for the auditions.

"Would you like something to drink?" he asked.

"I'm really excited about this—thanks so much for having me."

She was trying to stay focused, but she couldn't stop thinking about Ami and Fabienne. In the room was the Fricassee crew, along with a few other people Bale didn't recognize—they were also here for the audition. Roman introduced them to each other, and she said hi to the crew, nervously. She pulled Roman aside.

"Wait, was Ami here for the audition, too?"

"Sorry, pal," Roman said.

"Did he already go?"

"You're the last one."

He sat down on a plastic green chair, grabbing a piece of paper from the floor.

"Let's just do a jam session for right now—just play along with whatever you feel, and then after that, we can try out a few songs."

"Perfect," Bale said.

"You'll rock it out, for sure."

Bale appreciated Roman's welcoming nature, but inside she was burning with anger and frustration to the point that she had already started sweating.

Why couldn't he just join The Roux Roux Dolls with Fabienne? Fricassee wasn't what he was going for—so why?

"You ready?" Roman said.

Bale took in a deep breath and nodded.

One of the guitarists—Cheyanne—started them off, and then came the drums—Carlos—and the bass—Henri. The second guitarist— Dominique—started to play, and Andre was on the triangle. Roman went up to the mic and started singing while playing on the keyboard. The room was shaking.

Focus. Focus.

Bale started to tap her foot and move her head in rhythm—it didn't take her too long to become hypnotized, and she played the fiddle as she had never played before. Normally, she would stand in one spot and play, but for the audition, she was moving around, maneuvering her body along with the music—she was taken away in the moment, not in reality, and it was all a blur to her. As she played, memories of learning to play drifted in of herself in the backyard with her dad teaching her how to string the fiddle. Her mother, on the porch, slapping her knee with one hand while she's singing to the chickens in the front yard. And Bale herself playing her first show, where there were only a few people in the audience. She played and she played and she played until she was out of breath. When she stopped and came back to reality—her breathing the only sound in the room—she saw everyone in the room looking at her.

An applause.

"Wow," Roman said.

Bale tried to ease the movement of her chest.

"You just went for ten minutes straight after we stopped playing."

"Really?"

She looked around, seeing Ami and Fabienne in the back of the room. She wondered if they had watched her play.

Fabienne was smiling—Ami, his mouth wide open.

"That was magical," Roman said. "Why don't you take a quick break—maybe go outside a bit, before we start playing a few songs."

He patted her on the back.

"Well done, really."

Bale went outside to gather herself, pacing back and forth in the front yard. Her heavy breathing finally slowed down—her shirt, still soaked. She heard the door open.

Please, not now.

She turned around—Fabienne had stepped outside, walking toward her with a huge smile on her face.

"You rocked it," she said.

Bale didn't know how to respond—she didn't want to respond.

Walking in circles, she entered a vision of sitting next to Fabienne in the classroom, drawing Teenage Mutant Ninja Turtles on each other's arithmetic sheets. She remembered that Raphael was Fabienne's favorite. She sighed.

"You think so?"

"No doubt."

"It's still Raphael, right?"

"You know it—Donatello?"

Bale couldn't help but smile, and nodded.

"I've been here since the first audition," Fabienne said. "I would be shocked if you didn't get it."

Bale looked at the door.

"What about Ami?"

She laughed.

"He was good—but really, I don't think anyone could top what you just did. I've never seen anything like that."

Bale was feeling a bit better about herself, and about talking to Fabienne—someone she thought she'd never find comfort from. It made her miss the days of when they were at school together.

"Why didn't he just join Roux Roux? I don't get why he's trying for Fricassee. It would've been a better fit with you all."

"I know," Fabienne said.

"He knew I'd be going for this spot."

"I know."

"So why?"

"I don't know."

"I know," Bale said. "I definitely know the reason why."

Bale thought about it for a second, wondering if she should get into it—she had switched to walking back and forth again, all within the length of four feet.

"First, he cheats on me with you," she said. "Then I break up with him, but he still finds a way to keep being in my life, and he shows up here, knowing full well that I'll be here."

"Oh—please, Bale. Wait—about us—"

Before she could finish her words, Roman opened the door.

"You ready, Bale?"

"Sure."

"Let's do it," Roman said.

Bale played better when she was angry—she didn't care that Ami and Fabienne were standing in the back of the room while she auditioned with Fricassee. She would look up from time to time, seeing that he was moving his head to the music—making eye contact with her. The more she looked at him—the more he stood there in awe—the angrier she became, and her performance became stronger and stronger with each song they played.

The audition ended, and Bale saw Fabienne give her a thumbs up.

"That was amazing, Bale," Roman said, patting her on the shoulder. The rest of the band agreed with him, but Bale couldn't get herself to smile, though she thanked them for the opportunity. Roman hugged her and said that they'd get in touch soon about the band.

"Thanks for showing up," he said.

Without looking at Ami or Fabienne, she walked straight to the door, still breathing hard. Trying to remember how she played on her way home, it was all a blur to her. Only snippets popped into her head, and she tried to mouth the words from Roman or Fabienne, trying to make herself feel confident about the audition.

Bale's daydream of the audition, as she sat there in front of the Vermilion, was broken by a loud honk coming from the bridge above. She looked around to gain a sense of her whereabouts.

"Cut," she said.

That was the word—"cut"—she couldn't get it out of her head, hearing it from Roman the day before. That day, Bale made sure not to do anything—she kept the phone by her side at all times, basically staying in bed and watching TV at her parents' home, knowing that the decisions were going to be made that day.

When the phone finally rang—around seven at night—after a day's worth of impatience and anxiety, Bale put the TV on mute and immediately got out of bed. As usual, she started walking in circles in her room, making the wooden floors creak in rhythm.

"Sorry for taking so long," Roman said.

"Oh it's good," Bale replied. "I know how it goes."

"I'm so sorry, Bale, I really am but we—"

She sat back down on her bed, the glow of the TV shining on her face, and the posture of her shadow against the wall sank. The words sounded muffled to her—almost muffled, coming in bits as she stared at her own lap, fiddling with the blanket. It was so much that Roman was speaking unclearly—it was what he was saying that made her tune in and out.

"Difficult—direction—sorry—Ami—future—maybe—thank you—."

There was a pause before Bale realized that she was supposed to talk—that he had finished speaking—that the conversation required her to respond.

"Oh. Okay. Thank you for the opportunity. Really."

She felt sick and started to sweat—a different sweat from when she played a show. She leaned back onto the bed and covered her face with her blanket, trying to quiet her crying so that her parents wouldn't hear. Taking deep breaths to soften the sounds, her chest in constant stress.

When it was all done—after her emotions flowed and diminished, she looked at her phone and saw a message from Ami. *Sorry you didn't make the cut*, it read, and that was the last of her phone as she threw it against the wall. She watched the pieces splatter on the floor, and silence overtook the room as the bits of her phone stopped rolling around. It was soon after when Bale's dad walked in.

"What happened?" he asked. "Are you okay, sweet-pop?"

"Daddy," she said.

And Bale tried to explain what happened, but the words became disguised in her anger and frustration—breaking down again. Her dad rushed over and hugged her, asking what was wrong—Bale dug her face into his chest, trying not to cry, but the harder she tried, the faster the tears came.

"It's okay—it's okay, sweet-pop," he said, rubbing her back. "It's okay, Bale—it's okay."

The tears stopped, and she turned her face, still against her father's chest. He continued to console his daughter, rubbing her back and the back of her head. Bale lifted back her head and sat back—still sniffling, she explained to her dad what happened. He listened and empathized.

"Would you like me to give some thoughts?" he asked. "Or did you just want me to listen, sweet-pop?"

Just by hearing his voice, she felt calm—she felt like she was just a child—so many times her face had been tucked into her dad's chest.

"What are your thoughts?" she replied.

"Knowing you, sweet-pop, I think this will lead to even better and stronger opportunities. This will just make you more determined. Stronger. And to be honest, that band made the wrong decision, and their wrong decision is the right move for you. I promise."

"Ami," Bale said. "His message killed me. *Sorry you didn't make the cut.*"

"Well, sweet-pop," he said. "Fuck him—he shouldn't even be a thought in your head."

Bale looked at her dad's face—he was grinning, and she smiled.

"There's that twinkle," he said. "Let's go to IHOP and get some pancakes. I'll tell Mom that we'll be home late."

Bale sniffled and used the blanket to wipe her face.

"I'll be down in a bit, Daddy."

It was hot, but Bale didn't mind it, as she quietly laughed to herself thinking about that night with her dad at IHOP. They were there for two hours—he had seven pancakes and drowned them in syrup, butter, and whipped cream, along with hash browns, sunny-side-up eggs, and bacon. She ordered her favorite—two sunny-side-up eggs, French toast, and a Belgian waffle. Her dad lied to the waiter and said that it was Bale's birthday, and they were able to get a free ice cream sundae. She thought about how hard she slept last night—immediately drifting away as soon as she closed her eyes.

Last night seemed forever ago to Bale, having gone through so many emotions. She listened to the river and picked up her fiddle, and she started to play—it was a slow song, a tempo she usually didn't practice. With her head tilted—the Vermilion diagonal across her vision—she closed her eyes and let the strings sing a sad song to the river. Drenched in sweat, the air humid and heavy, Bale felt comfortable—in a dream or a lullaby, she felt at peace for the first time in a long time. When she finished, she opened her eyes, and on the other side of the river, she saw a lamb looking at her.

"Best audience ever," she said.

"Magical," Fabienne said. "As always—that was amazing."

Bale turned her head around—Fabienne was holding an acoustic guitar. She turned her head back around, not speaking.

"Can I sit with you?"

She didn't respond.

"Please, Bale."

Bale stood up and brushed the grass off and started to walk away, but Fabienne pleaded for her to stop.

"Donatello, please, wait."

She stopped.

"What?"

"Come back, please—just sit with me."

"Why? All you do is lie and cheat—literally."

"That's not fair, Bale."

"Fair?"

She laughed in disbelief.

"What's not fair? Fucking my boyfriend while we were still together? Oh. I'm sorry. I'm sorry that you fucked my boyfriend while we were still together, and I wasn't happy about it, and I didn't support you and him cheating on me. I'm so sorry, Fabienne. I'm sorry about that, and that it's unfair that I'm mad at you because you lied and fucked my Ami while we were still together. My apologies, Fabienne."

"Wait—that's not what I meant."

"What's not fair then?"

"Nothing," she said. "I didn't mean that. I know. I didn't mean that you were being unfair."

"But you meant to fuck Ami, right?"

Fabienne took a deep breath and sat in the grass, putting her guitar next to her.

"You still got the grit, don't you," she said. "Good. Always keep that grit, Bale."

Bale heard her father's voice in her head—the lamb across the river was chewing grass, and she felt calm again.

"I'm sorry," Fabienne said. "For it all—I'm sorry for it all. I promise."

Bale walked up to her, but she didn't sit down.

"Why are you here?"

"Ami told me you'd be here—he said it's your favorite spot."

"Why are you here?"

"I want to play with you?"

Bale saw themselves playing on the swing sets at school.

"Play."

"I want to play with you," Fabienne said. "Come sit. Please."

She continued to stand—overhead, a flock of birds were flying—they vanished into the sun, and the lamb was gone, but she could hear it bleating in the distance.

"I didn't know," Fabienne said. "I didn't know that you and Ami were still together at the time. I thought that you all had broken up."

Bale kept her distance, but she sat down.

"It wasn't until later I found out," she continued. "And I was mad at Ami—I went off on him."

This made Bale feel better.

"But what we have is nothing big, Bale—it really isn't genuine. I promise."

"I get it," Bale replied.

"And look—to be honest, I don't expect this to last, and I'm sure he'll find someone else or I'll find someone else. It's just for right now. He just wants to get his music label—that's all he wants."

Fabienne laughed.

"I'm bi, anyway—who knows, maybe we can get together and get back at him one day."

This made Bale smile.

"I wanted to kill him," she said. "This message he sent last night about not making the cut—"

"I know," Fabienne interrupted. "I saw it. I've already taken care of that."

They were both drenched in sweat. Fabienne wiped her forehead.

"Don't worry about Fricassee," she said. "You need to form your own band. No group right now can handle you—you're too good, too powerful. That's all, Bale—they're just scared."

Bale couldn't get herself to still be mad at her. It was even harder for her to remain angry as memories of them being friends at school flowed in and out. Bale moved a bit closer to Fabienne and picked up her fiddle and started to play the same song she had been stringing when Fabienne first arrived. Fabienne picked up her acoustic guitar and started to strum it—together, like they were Donatello and Raphael from years ago—they were in harmony, and the Vermilion River flowed and listened.

Frog Creek Crow

As it grew—just past the broken crawfish hut and around the turn of the curve where the splintered bridge crossed Frog Creek Crow—down at the end of the Chavaniac cul-de-sac, the magnolia tree, which was once large and alive and magnificent, had toppled over, broken in half, rotted and bare. Its branches, twigs—remnants—brown and cracked leaves scattered around, littering patches of grass and dirt, making Aristide feel tired. He stood on the front of his porch in his underwear, one hand rubbing his stomach, the other scratching his thigh. It was morning, but his forehead had already gathered sweat as the humidity had settled in from the rains the night before.

Behind him, under the creaking ceiling fan, a straw chair—seventeen years old, which he had made when he was just a child, an apprentice of his dad who was a carpenter by trade. A hard-working man Aristide's father was, playing an important role in his life before he had passed away two years ago in March. Aristide remembered his father as a kind, gentle person—one who avoided arguments by telling stories—and through those tales, many lessons Aristide had learned whether it was at the time or later on in his life. Not once could Aristide remember his dad raising his voice or expressing any frustration and anger.

The broken magnolia before him—he remembered sitting with his father on the porch on particularly windy days, watching the thriving magnolia tree lose its flowers, floating and whispering away into the sky.

"They'll come back," his father would say, every time. "Before you know it, they'll be back glittering our tree like it was meant to be."

And he would sip on his iced tea—Aristide, his lemonade—until the mosquitoes came out in full force, which meant it was dinner time. When it rained, his dad would stick out his glass to get one drop of rain. "Got to love the sky, son," he would say every time.

For dinner, red beans and rice were the staples in their household, and neither Aristide nor his father became tired of it.

"Simple, and to the point, and it gets the job done," his dad would say, laughing. "Much like me, I'd like to think."

Aristide himself had eventually perfected his dad's red beans and rice. "It's always in the timing," his dad said. "Everything is in its timing."

It had taken Aristide some time, but through many attempts of tasting and failing, he was able to eventually find the savory tint to his cooking.

The day before his dad died, as they sat on the porch and as the magnolia tree released its bloom into the air, Aristide's father didn't speak or say his usual phrase. He remained quiet. And Aristide remained quiet.

And the next morning, just before breakfast, he found his dad dead on the floor, just next to the bed his father and his mother had slept in for years—the certain number, Aristide didn't know. He didn't know how long they were together. He didn't know how long they were married and for how long they were married before he was born. He didn't know much about his mother.

Early in their marriage, she left them, not giving any explanation, four years after she had given birth to their son. He couldn't remember his mother much—how she looked, the sound of her voice, the clothes she wore—just vague shadows flickered as he tried to remember her. He created images of her—long dark hair, watery eyes, tanned skin, wearing a long yellow dress. Her voice—soft and welcoming, and she had a loud laugh. He knew that these memories that he had made for himself were bits and pieces from mothers of his friends or other people he knew.

Aristide's father never talked about Sidonie, but there were times, Aristide could tell, that Avit wanted to, or that he was thinking about her—as at rare times at night, when his father thought he was sleeping, Aristide would be awake listening to his dad cry in the next room. Sometimes, he would see his father looking through old photos—pictures his dad would never show him. Her clothes were still neatly kept in the dresser, and when he fixed the bed in the mornings, he would always puff up her pillow.

As he stood there on the porch, still looking at the snapped magnolia, he thought about the morning Avit died.

"Dad," Aristide said, looking down at him on the floor. He nudged him a few times before turning him over so that he faced the ceiling. His chest wasn't moving. He was wearing his favorite plaid shirt—one that, Aristide had assumed, was a gift from Sidonie. Aristide ran outside of his house, across three fields before reaching the nearest neighbor. When Lilia opened the door, Aristide was out of breath. He leaned over panting.

"What's wrong, honey?" Lilia asked. "Would you like something to drink?"

Just behind her, brushing against her legs was a pup—a chocolate Labrador. As Aristide continued to breathe hard, he looked into the eyes of the dog and felt an unexpected sensation of love.

"Dad," Aristide said.

He shook his head, and Lilia ran to the phone, while Aristide stayed at the front door. He could hear her talking, but it was muffled—the world to Aristide was muffled as he just tilted his head and looked into the watery eyes of the Labrador pup. He reached out his hand, and she licked his fingertips, looking sad.

"So simple," he said.

Lilia rushed back from the kitchen to the front door, and in one motion she swooped up the pup and grabbed Aristide by the arm.

"Come on, Sunshine," she said.

Aristide almost fell as she pulled him by his hand.

"They're coming," she said. "I'll drive you back."

They got into a red truck—Sunshine sat on Aristide's lap. Lilia put down the windows and revved the engine before screeching out of the driveway.

"I just wish," Lilia said. "I just wish that Avit kept a phone at the house—specifically for reasons like this."

Aristide thought about the conversation he had with his dad about how he didn't like using phones, but he only liked to talk to people in person.

"It's the faces, son," he once told Aristide. "The faces tell you every story you need to know."

Aristide gently rubbed the top of Sunshine's head—Lilia lit a cigarette and took two long puffs before throwing it out the window.

"Is he dead, honey?"

"I think so."

"Oh, honey."

Lilia almost ran into the front of their house, just breaking at the front of the porch—next to the truck was the majestic magnolia tree. Lilia ran inside, but Aristide remained, whispering to Sunshine as tears came down his face.

There was the burial.

He was buried as requested, between his two dogs, who had passed away before Aristide was born. The hallways of their house were covered in framed photos of the two dogs, and Aristide knew how important it was to his dad to be buried with them.

After the funeral, Aristide took over his dad's business. It wasn't easy for him—though he had learned much under his dad's mentoring, he knew he lacked both the experience and the confidence to maintain the business as his father had done. Errors in measurements, the wrong supplies, forgotten tools, broken materials, living on his own—these were just some of the obstacles Aristide had faced as he learned the trade.

There were times where he would just sit on his dad's bed and cry, much like Avit had done when he was thinking about Sidonie. There were times he wanted to quit it all and just work at Lilia's restaurant, boiling crawfish and shrimp. It was the magnolia tree that kept him going, knowing how much Avit had loved it—his love for the magnolia and the conversations they had on the porch about the tree were embedded in Aristide's soul, memories that only became stronger as time passed.

The city of Lafayette helped him out—those who lived nearby and those who lived across town, all who had known Avit and had watched Aristide grow up since he was born supported him. Especially when he was young, but even when he was a teenager, Aristide practically lived at various businesses and homes as his father worked at these places, becoming friends with his clients and their children, being fed onsite, and even being scolded when he was in trouble—they were all uncles and aunts to him. Though much work could have been done by the owners themselves—whether it was their own houses or businesses—they wanted to make sure Aristide would be financially secure, and not only that, but to keep him busy to avoid thinking about the passing of his father—shops, houses, sheds, tractors, gardens and the like gave Aristide purpose during a time when he felt lost. Even other carpenters helped him, suggesting to some of their customers that they should reach out to Aristide instead.

He worked nonstop for two years, nothing but routine—breakfast, work, lunch, work, dinner, sleep. Red beans and rice every day, and every now and then, the local folks would drop by to keep him company. He learned the trade and became a strong carpenter, but as his life settled into normalcy again, and during those nights alone at his home, Aristide struggled with his thoughts.

It didn't surprise him, on one night, that he had contemplated taking his own life, though the idea had never entered his mind until that day, and as he opened one of the kitchen drawers and took out a knife, then faced the opened window which gave way to the backyard—sprinkled with hibiscuses, azaleas, and irises—he closed his eyes and saw himself in his father's lap. A voice came to him—a voice he felt like he should remember, singing a lullaby which he wasn't sure he had heard before. The tune made him open his eyes and put the knife back in the drawer, and from that night on, he never slept in his own room or on his father's bed or in the house at all, but in the back patio, on a hammock which stretched from one oak to another—shielded from the sky with a wooden roof Avit had made years ago. But whether he was in the house or outside in the backyard, Aristide didn't get much sleep since the passing of Avit—long nights awake, red eyes, too tired to shower or cut his fingernails—Aristide's way of life had completely transformed into a mode of stagnant numbing sensations where he failed to take care of himself.

Regionally Catholic, still Aristide didn't know much about church and God and praying, and after the night in the kitchen, he set himself on his knees bedside, clasped his hands and closed his eyes and tried to pray. He tried to pray but he didn't know how to—his words and his thoughts went everywhere except to his intentions.

"What do I do?" he whispered, eyes tightly closed.

He opened them.

"What do I say?"

He left it at that.

So on that morning, Aristide, as he stood there on the porch and looked at the forlorn tree, wondered what his father would've done with it—he wondered what happened, how he could've let the magnolia fall apart as it did. He was too focused on the business, not noticing the withering magnolia.

"It's my fault," he said.

He lit a cigarette—a habit he had developed only recently—and took in a deep breath.

"I'm sorry, Dad," he said. "I'm so tired. I miss you."

He barely washed up, and it took all of his energy to brush his teeth. Putting on some jeans and his favorite T-shirt—a faded green cloth with a yellow imprint of an owl, gifted to him by Avit—he walked alongside

Frog Creek Crow and followed its path to the coulee. It was a quiet morning where only the melodies of birds and the rushed sounds of the squirrels rustling through a line of trees could be heard. He counted how many pieces of trash he passed as he walked. There—at the coulee—as always, was Grinnie, sitting on a patch of grass amid dirt with a fishing rod and a boombox. Don McLean's "American Pie" was playing, and Grinnie was gently singing along—Aristide crouched down next to him and listened. He continued to sing as he patted Aristide on the back, without looking at him. It didn't take too long for Aristide to join his friend, and their voices became louder and louder, smirking and laughing as they sang. When the song came to an end, Grinnie pressed the *Stop* button and then *Rewind*, still not saying any words to Aristide—he pressed *Play* and the song came on again. Aristide looked beyond the coulee where there was a bright green pasture—a few cows grazed, their hooves wet from the morning dew.

"This song and only this song, right Grinnie?"

He nodded his head.

"On repeat until I die."

"That should go on your grave."

"It better."

Grinnie lit a cigarette—taking a couple of puffs, he handed it over to Aristide and lit another one.

"You're in charge of that, Aris," he said. "When I go, you get that on my stone, and I'll be happy to be dead."

Aristide exhaled.

"I got you."

A hawk flew overhead—its wings spread wide as Aristide looked at it with one eye closed in the rising sun. It soared away until the blue sky engulfed its flight.

"Do you pray?" Aristide asked.

"What's that?" Grinnie said.

"Like do you pray?"

"What do you mean?"

"Folding your hands and bowing your head and all."

Grinnie puffed on his cigarette and took in a deep breath before exhaling. He spat.

"Yeah I pray. You?"

"I don't think I know how to."

"What do you mean?"

"I tried once, but I didn't know what to do."

Grinnie laughed.

"Just do what you just said—put your hands together and bow your head."

"And then what?"

"That's up to you—pray what you feel like praying for."

Aristide looked at the cows on the other side of the coulee—a calf standing next to its mother, he assumed.

"What do you pray for, Grinnie?"

"I don't know, you know. I just pray."

"Do you pray for me?"

"Sure I do, Aris," he said, patting him on the back.

"When I figure it out, I'm going to pray for you."

"I appreciate that."

Without missing a beat, he started singing along again. Aristide listened to him, in unison with McLean—he admired his friend's voice, and he would always try to get him to play in front of a crowd, but Grinnie kept his talents to himself.

"You can get real big," Aristide once said.

"I want to be small."

When the song finished, Grinnie rewound the tape and played it again.

"You think my mom is still around?" Aristide asked.

"I do, Aris," Grinnie said, as if he had been wondering about it just as much as Aristide.

He hummed along to the song.

"I think I want to find her."

Grinnie put the volume down but not all the way down.

"I wouldn't be surprised if she lived somewhere nearby."

"Really?"

Grinnie spat and nodded his head.

"How do I find her?"

"The library."

"What's that?"

"The library."

"How?"

Aristide combed the dirt with his fingers.

"Through the desktop computers."

Grinnie lit another cigarette and gave it to Aristide, who had made a mound out of the dirt—he patted it softly.

"They have desktop computers we can use—you know Charlotte?"

"I know Charlotte," Aristide said.

He thought about her red hair and freckles.

"She can help you out. One time I went to the library, and she helped me find a spark plug on the Internet. I ordered it and everything—maybe you can look your mom up."

Aristide felt his chest tighten—nervous.

"Maybe it's not a good idea."

Grinnie spat and put his arm around Aristide's shoulder. He hummed for a bit.

"I get it," he said. "But maybe think about it. Or at least you know it's there if you want to look for her."

"You think I should?"

"Sometimes I put myself in your life, especially over the past couple of years, and I think I would do it. I'm not saying that you should do it, but I would—I would want to find her."

The two remained silent and listened to "American Pie" a few more times, chain smoking and watching the cows under the sun.

"I got to get," Grinnie said.

"Yeah."

"Look," Grinnie said.

He pointed down the road and gave him the directions. It was in the part of town that Aristide wasn't too familiar with, but he figured that he could walk it.

"About thirty-five minutes by the way you walk," Grinnie said.

He gave Aristide the rest of his cigarettes and the lighter, and after a hug, Aristide took off for the library. It wasn't so much that Aristide minded the distance of the walk, meaning the physical exertion of it, but it was more the amount of time it gave him to think about Sidonie. He still wasn't sure if he really wanted to find her or search for her. What if she was still around? What if she moved across the country, or what if she was already dead? What would you say to her? Would you meet with her—his mind was full of thoughts, those that had never entered before.

"Sidonie," he whispered over and over to himself, hoping that just by saying her name, it would help him to make his decision.

As he went on his way, he waved at every truck driving by and counted every piece of trash he passed—he lost count at times and started over. Sometimes he counted every bird he saw or the dead opossums, armadillos, and squirrels on the road. Occasionally, he was offered a ride—sometimes by acquaintances, other times by strangers—but he declined on both as he wanted to focus on his thoughts.

Aristide was drenched in sweat by the time he arrived at the library, but he didn't take much notice of it. He was nervous as he walked in and looked around, feeling overwhelmed—there was a line at the front desk, but beyond, he saw a row of computers. The musk of the books caused his allergies to act up—watery eyes—and it didn't take too long for him to sniffle. He sneezed, standing in front of a computer—a tap on his shoulder.

"I've been meaning to get in touch," Charlotte said.

Aristide tucked in his stomach and stood up straight. Seeing Charlotte made him more nervous. He wiped his nose.

"It's been awhile," he said.

"I'm so sorry."

"Monkey bars," Aristide said.

They had gone to grade school together—being good friends back then—but when Charlotte changed schools after fifth grade, they hadn't kept in touch. Aristide thought about the playground—a massive castle made of wood. He spent most of his time on the monkey bars, and talking to Charlotte took him back to one particular day during recess. He was swinging on the bars, but the blisters on his palms were too painful and he fell, landing on his back—making it hard for him to breathe. Once he was able to open his eyes from the pain, he saw Charlotte's face peering over him.

"Are you bleeding?"

Aristide coughed, trying to breathe.

"Are you hurt?"

Again, he couldn't answer.

"You look hurt."

Aristide lifted his head and then put it back against the ground—he took in deep breaths and coughed.

"I don't know," he managed to say.

A bump on the back of his head had already formed—he felt its pressure as his head throbbed.

"Do you want my Fruit Roll-Ups?" Charlotte asked.

Tears came down his face though he wasn't crying.

"We can trade," he said. "I have a Chocolate Swiss Roll."

A small crowd had formed around him, and eventually one of the teachers came and gave the help that he needed.

"I remember that," Charlotte said. "That seems like forever ago."

"It was the best Fruit Roll-Ups I ever ate."

"I'm glad you're okay," she said, laughing.

Her mood took a serious tone.

"I'm really sorry," she said. "I really meant to get in touch, but you know, with work and all, and I have two kids—it has been nonstop."

"It's great to see you," Aristide said.

He looked at the computer.

"Do you need some help?" Charlotte asked.

"I do."

He told her.

"Oh," Charlotte said.

She looked down at the carpet.

"Sidonie. This might be the first time I've heard you mention her name."

"She has been on my mind lately."

Charlotte paused, still not looking at Aristide, and sat down in front of the computer, pulling up a chair for him next to her.

She logged in using her account—as she typed, Aristide looked at her freckles, freckles he hadn't seen in years—it reminded him of home.

Aristide didn't know his mother's maiden name, and they tried a variety of terms in the search engine. *Sidonie. Sidonie Lafayette La. Sidonie Guidry. Sidonie Obituary. Sidonie Obituary Louisiana. Avit Guidry and Sidonie. Avit and Sidonie Wedding Lafayette.* Nothing of use came through—they looked at the images, but there weren't any pictures related to Sidonie.

"She's done well in staying hidden," Charlotte said.

"I guess it's for the best," Aristide said.

"I'll keep looking for you, and I'll definitely let you know if I find anything."

"Either way—drop by anytime. You know the address."

"I do."

They hugged—he wanted to kiss her on the cheek.

"Take care, Aristide the Glide—I'll see you soon."

Aristide didn't go straight home from the library—he took a slight detour and headed over to Frog Creek Crow, where he had a favorite spot in the shade under a row of pecan trees. He took off his shirt and lay in the grass, the sun peeking through the branches. A few pecans were around him, and he cracked some against each other to eat. The long walks and the sun had gotten to him, and he closed his eyes—when he woke up, it was evening.

"Mom," he whispered as he gained his bearings. "Dad."

He found himself in a dark world again—his thoughts haunted him as they had done that one night in the kitchen. He took off his shoes, his jeans, and stripped naked, then entered the water, kneeling down. The frogs were loud—the creek, in its rhythm—a song for anyone who listened. Aristide listened. He lunged forward face first into the water and closed his eyes—flashes of his past seeped in—clasping his hands, he closed his eyes tighter and held his breath for as long as he could, the water hushed the world for him. He pushed himself back up, exhaling and breathing hard and loud. The frogs were still there—Aristide listened.

He walked home half naked, not going inside—he sat on the porch, pretending that his dad was there sitting in the chair next to him.

Just as the mosquitoes were making their way and as the sun came down, Aristide saw a shadow walking toward his house. He let the mosquitoes take his blood as he waited for the stranger to arrive. The sky was darker than usual, signaling rain.

Closer and closer. Aristide waited. He tried to make sense of the slow-walking person.

"Dad?" he said. "Dad?"

Soon enough he realized that the person wasn't his dad but a lady. She walked up, wearing a sunhat and sunglasses, though the sun was gone by the time she arrived.

"Hello, ma'am," Aristide said.

She took off her glasses and looked at Aristide, looking like she wanted to smile. Her voice was strong and vibrant.

"Sorry, honey," she said. "I'm a bit late."

Aristide looked at her eyes and lips and chin. He thought that she looked so familiar.

"I don't know you," he said. "But you look like someone I know."

"I know," the lady replied.

She turned around and looked at the magnolia tree.

"It has been awhile," she said. "Looks like that tree needs a bit of mending."

Aristide looked at the tree and then at her again.

"Let's get you inside before the mosquitoes take your bones," she said. "The clouds are coming, too."

"Yes, ma'am," Aristide said.

In the kitchen, the lady took out the kettle and two mugs to make some tea. She knew where everything was kept. Only the sounds of the clattering and clanging of tin and porcelain and wood filled the room as Aristide watched in silence. She reminded him of his dad.

She sat down in front of Aristide.

"Mother," Aristide said.

"Son."

"Why'd you leave?"

"I know."

"Why?"

Sidonie rubbed her hands against the wood of the table.

"It's been really tough, you know."

"I'm here. I'm here forever."

"You're here, right?"

"I'm here."

She stood and walked over to the stove—the kettle was getting ready to whistle.

"We're here, Aristide. And we'll turn that magnolia back into magic, and we'll be okay."

"Yes, Mother."

The kettle started to sing, and Sidonie sang along—a lullaby, a lullaby that Aristide once heard before. And the rain started to come down.

Redfish

HE WAS KNOWN as Skittles, and every evening and sometimes on Saturday mornings, he'd stand on the corner of South Meyers Street—just outside the Circle K on Kaliste Saloom, one of Lafayette's busiest streets—smoking a cigarette while leaning against the broken tire pressure machine.

Odilon didn't know why they called him Skittles for the longest time, but whenever he'd pop into the store to get his daily cup of coffee and a mini-pack of Oreos, the cashier would look out the window and laugh, saying "There goes that Skittles—at it again every day" as he shook his head.

Sometimes Odilon would see people walk up to him, and he'd take something out of his pocket and there would be an exchange of some sort, but it never looked like any money was being handed over—a quick handshake or a hug, and then he would see them putting something in their pockets.

It could be storming—it could be 100 degrees or a windy 30 degrees and no matter what, he'd be there, leaning on that tire pressure machine— Odilon was amazed at how he could light a cigarette and keep it going on those rainy, windy days.

Odilon knew that Skittles was a gambler. He played the slots, or poker, or the tracks—he put money on games, the fights mainly, and though he usually always came out on top, no one would know it. Clothed in a white shirt and khakis, always—no matter the weather, and a red Ragin' Cajuns hat, he kept his life simple. He went all over Louisiana to get the edge—to squeeze as much as he could out of the gambling game.

Odilon himself kept his life simple, too. After being in and out of jail for misdemeanors, he was able to settle down as a barista for one of the local coffee shops—The Cafe, off St. Mary's, just a block down from his apartment. The owner, Blue, knew all about Odilon's lifestyle because he lived it himself once, and that was how Odilon was able to get another chance at some kind of job security. The coffee shop was also a bar, so he worked double shifts as much as possible, especially Friday and Saturday nights. The more he worked, the less of a chance that he would fall back into his previous ways. That was all to his life now—working and staying home, watching TV or drawing or listening to music and hanging out with Ma. He happily had no friends, having cut off anyone from those days he would find himself in constant trouble. It felt strange to him—not worrying about committing any crimes or wondering about food or clothes, a life that had consumed him since he left his house at the age of eighteen.

His parents? His parents were kind and caring—relentless with their love for their son. Odilon knew this, too—but he was too stubborn, becoming caught up in a lifestyle influenced by the group of friends he had surrounded himself with, friends who also wanted their own freedom and responsibility but not knowing how to live this way without getting themselves in trouble. They all fed off each other, being bad because they were trying to prove something when they had nothing to prove—getting caught up with the idea that they didn't need to live like the upper middle-class families they grew up with—rebellious antics because they thought they knew it all.

The conversations on the phone with his Ma, when he called from time to time, were what got to him the most.

"Come home, Baby O," Ma said. "Come get a hot dinner and sleep in your bed. We miss you."

"I know, Ma."

"Your dad misses you. He hasn't been the same since you left and hearing how you've been living."

"I know, Ma."

"Call him. We love you and want you to be happy."

"I know, Ma."

"Do you still have a key?"

"Yeah, Ma."

"We'll be going out of town this weekend—why don't you just come here and stay a couple of days while we're out, just for a couple of days? There's some redfish your dad caught the other day. I'll cook it up and spice it up and keep it in the fridge for you."

"I got to go, Ma."

"It'll be just how you like it."

"I got to go, Ma."

"Okay, Baby O."

"I'll call again."

It pained Odilon—every time he hung up the phone with Ma, feeling guilty, knowing that she and his dad were the only two people in the world who truly loved him. Knowing that he didn't treat them the way he knew how they should be treated.

"I'm such a brat," he would say every time.

When they went out of town that weekend, Odilon went by the house. He ate the fish and washed the few clothes he had and took cash from Ma's secret little canister that she kept tucked away under her bed behind empty shoeboxes. He thought about all of the times she would take money from it and give it to him when he was young.

"This is my own personal savings," she would say. "I save it for you."

He cried when he left the house, full of anger—at himself for the way he had led his life and how he treated his parents. He knew, though, how happy they would be knowing that he dropped by and ate the redfish.

Not long after that last phone call, shortly after the weekend his parents returned from their trip, Odilon's dad passed away. Memories swarmed Odilon's head as he hid in the back during the funeral—particularly ones when he and his dad would be fishing at the river. His dad, showing him how to set the pole and the rhythm of the sway, letting the reel go and hearing it whirl.

"Now you got to listen, son," Pa said.

"Listen to what?" Odilon replied.

"Now you got to listen to the muddy banks—they'll sing about the fish."

Odilon shifted his head to see through the crowd before him, his mother's face, who would turn her head back from time to time—he knew she was looking for him.

"Daddy, where do the fish swim to—where are they going?"

"They're going to the end of the world, son."

He remembered his soft voice—his gentle skin and how he always walked like he was never going anywhere, like he was surprised whenever he reached wherever he was going. It was the small delights in life his dad treasured that Odilon remembered the most—how he was always amazed to see the sun in the morning and the moon at night.

"Hi, Ma," he whispered to himself as the service had ended.

That night he couldn't stop thinking about Ma, living alone after being with his dad for fifty-four years.

"I was there, Ma," Odilon said. "I'm sorry, Ma."

"I know, Baby O," Ma said. "I know you were there."

"You saw me?"

"I saw you, Baby O."

"Are you going to be okay, Ma?"

"Do you have food to eat tonight?" she asked.

Odilon twirled the cord—he was at Mel's Diner, using their phone. The restaurant was becoming crowded—the bar crowd was just coming in after a night's drinking until closing time.

"It's getting loud here, Ma," he said. "I'll call soon."

After hanging up the phone, he met his group of friends outside and they walked toward the pawn shop. This was Odilon's last stint before he changed his life. It all took place after being arrested for breaking into the store.

It was during his first night in jail—he had to spend the weekend there—when he started to think about Ma and how she was all by herself and how scared and lonely she must have been. He realized, as he looked at his orange clothing and the scratch mark on his elbow he got while climbing over the railing of the bunk bed, not wanting to awaken the man who was sleeping below him, that he didn't want this life anymore even though it meant leaving all that he'd known for the past five years. He wanted to know his Ma again. He wanted clean clothes and a steady job and a warm place to stay. He wanted to be a part of the world he once knew years ago.

He called Ma from jail, telling her that he would be home soon.

"Okay, Baby O," she said. "Just let me know when, and I'll have some pecan pie for you."

"I'll be home, Ma," he said. "And we'll be okay."

He didn't tell her that he was in jail, but he gathered that she knew just from having to accept the phone call from the correctional center automated system.

The weekend was long for Odilon, more so than his previous times, knowing that he was going to change his life for the better—knowing that he was going home. Finally the day arrived—he made bail with the help of a friend, one whom he had known since childhood. He hadn't talked to him in years, since high school, but he never forgot his phone number, one that he had called a million times during their friendship.

He waited outside of the correctional center and saw that his friend was still driving the same car.

"I can't believe you still drive this," Odilon said as he opened the door.

"It's been awhile," Cairo said.

"My fault. Thank you so much for this. You look good."

"You, too."

It didn't take them long to get back on track with their friendship— like they had been talking to each other for the past five years, laughing and catching up on the past.

"You going to be okay?" Cairo asked as he pulled into Ma's driveway.

"I might need your help, but yeah, we're going to be okay."

"Sorry again about your dad."

They hugged and Odilon tapped on the trunk of the car before Cairo pulled out and drove off.

The transition from street-life back to home-life had little setbacks, mainly dealing with restlessness and missing the adrenaline rush of his previous day-to-day living, but whenever he thought about those days, all he had to do was look at Ma and talk to her for a bit as every time he did so, it reminded him of how much he loved her—how she was the only person in the world who loved him more than anyone else.

He had his withdrawals—drugs and alcohol—but he attended meetings, and sometimes Ma would go with him in support.

"Hi, my name is Odilon, and I'm an addict."

Ma's voice was the one that was always the loudest—the one he heard above everyone else.

"Hi, Baby O."

One night at the house, as he and Ma were going through some of his dad's belongings, Ma broke down.

"I'm so glad you're home, Baby O," she said, in tears.

"I know, Ma. I'm here now. We're good, Ma."

"I don't think I would've been able to make it all by myself, dear."

"I don't think I could've either, Ma."

They spent the rest of that night looking at old photos and boxing up his dad's clothes to donate to the local shelter. After they had finished, they sat in the back patio—the Lafayette humidity had stretched out, sticking to their skin, and the condensation from the glasses of their lemonades formed tiny puddles on the table they shared. Odilon wiped it off with one hand while he had a cigarette in the other. He made sure to puff away from Ma, though the smoke didn't drift too far as it seemed trapped in the thickness of the air.

"Those mosquitoes now, Baby O," Ma said. "They're getting bigger and bigger, just like the moon out there, plump and quiet."

"I know, Ma. They're biting tonight."

"Where you going to go, Baby O?"

"I'm not going anywhere, Ma—I'm right here. I'm right here with you."

"But where you going, Baby O?"

Odilon put out his cigarette and exhaled.

"You know I'm not going to be around much longer, Baby O," Ma said.

"Don't say that, Ma."

"I say that because I want to make sure you're going to be okay. That you'll be able to live on your own and take care of yourself."

"I won't have it any other way—I'll make it, Ma. I start my new job next week, too."

"You didn't tell me that," she said with excitement.

"Remember The Cafe? Remember Blue? Remember how you didn't like me going there when I should've been doing my homework and all during school?"

"I can't believe, Baby O."

"Strange how that works out—getting a second chance at The Cafe. Blue is a real good guy. He's looking out for me."

"That's really good, Baby O."

Ma rocked back in her chair, looking at the stars.

"What are you going to do after, Baby O? When I'm gone in the stars?"

"Oh Ma," Odilon said. "Let's not talk about that. Right now we have an infinity together just like that night sky."

"We do, don't we, Baby O."

They sat on the back patio for another hour or so before turning in—they traded stories about Odilon's dad, laughing and crying while the mosquitoes buzzed around, disguised in the twinkle of the stars.

Odilon had set himself a solid routine once he started his shifts at The Cafe. He mainly got the nights, especially on the weekends because most of the other employees wanted to enjoy their free time then. Blue had expanded The Cafe, which was once just a little coffee shop where teenagers hung out after school and smoked cigarettes and listened to the antique jukebox that could only play a few songs like Janis Joplin's

"Piece Of My Heart." That was why Ma didn't want Odilon to go there in his youth, thinking that he would just smoke his life away there and do nothing other than doing everything he wasn't supposed to be doing. But the coffee shop wasn't quite working after a while, business-wise, and Blue had to expand it into a bar as well, and he also started to serve food, like the usual kind of bar food. The Cafe was divided into two—one side being a cafe and the other room a bar with a pool table and one large TV mounted on the wall. Once that side of the business opened, Blue was doing well again with sales.

"I got to ask," Blue said.

They were at The Cafe—Odilon was training before his first shift.

"Are you going to be alright with all of the booze?"

"It's funny—on the cafe side, a lot of my friends from AA are there. I'm sure you know them by now—they've been coming for years. I should be okay—it's time now."

It didn't take too long for Odilon to catch on—figuring out how to make espresso drinks while also mixing cocktails and preparing sandwiches and washing dishes. He loved it, and for the first time in his life, he was proud of himself. During breaks, he'd sit down with his AA friends, laughing, drinking coffee, and they would go outside to smoke their cigarettes, much like Odilon had done when he went to The Cafe at a younger age.

One night—after a good shift, Odilon was working the bar when Skittles sat down at the counter and ordered his drink.

"Say," Odilon said as he was mixing shots. "Aren't you the one who hangs out down by the Circle K off Kaliste Saloom?"

Skittles shook his head and fixed his baseball cap.

"Sure is," he said.

"I see you there every day."

"That's me."

Skittles looked up at the TV screen—the Pelicans were playing the Bucks.

"I like to get my Oreos from there—I go there every morning, too."

"They have some good Oreos there now," Skittles said. "And that's a good group of people who work there."

"The best."

"Oh yeah—Rousseau and them. That's a good crew. They're always looking out for me."

Odilon put the drink down in front of him.

"They make me laugh—they're always arguing about something."

"Something and something," Skittles said. "Always something."

He laughed and took a sip.

"I was just wondering," Odilon said. "What do you do out there, next to the tire pump and all?"

"Oh nothing," Skittles said. "That's all—just nothing."

Odilon knew that meant that he didn't want to talk about it, so he nodded his head and smiled and watched the game. Not too much later, a man came and sat down next to Skittles, and Odilon could tell that they were good friends—talking about the game and joking around, pushing each other and cursing playfully.

"Well that's my shift," Odilon said. "I'll see you."

"You take good care now," Skittles said. "Enjoy them Oreos."

Odilon, though it was the first time he talked to Skittles, found himself looking up to him—admiring his demeanor and how it looked like he had life down just right.

"If I don't see you at the K, come back here again, and the next drink is on me."

"Deal," Skittles said.

Odilon was smiling as he drove back home, looking forward to telling Ma about meeting Skittles—he had told her about him and how he was always standing outside Circle K. He was feeling happy, and it wasn't like he wasn't happy after he had changed his life, but it was like a different feeling, one that arose from being social and enjoying the company of someone else, especially Skittles—a man he was curious about since he had started his routine of going to the Circle K in the mornings.

"Ma," he said, rushing into the door. "Guess what, Ma?"

"What's going on, Baby O? Are you okay, Baby O?"

"I met the man outside of Circle K—the legend himself, I met him."

He put his arms around Ma and hugged her—she hadn't seen her son so excited in a long time, since he was just a child walking into the arcade at the Acadiana Mall.

Ma started to cry.

"Why the tears, Ma? What's wrong, Ma?"

"I just haven't seen you so happy like this in a long time. It brings back some good memories, Baby O."

"I know, Ma."

He led her to the living room, and they sat down on the couch and Odilon told her all about his night and talking with Skittles at The Cafe. Ma was so happy for him—she barely understood what he was saying, but she would laugh and smile every time her son had done so.

But that was the last time Odilon saw Skittles at The Cafe. Last week, on a Saturday morning as Odilon pulled into the Circle K as usual—it was a sunny day, really pretty—Skittles was there as usual, and he was talking to a man in a red jacket. At first, Odilon was excited to see Skittles, and he was wondering if he should go say hi to him after he finished talking to the man in the red jacket, but he soon realized, as he pulled into a parking spot, that the man held a knife and he was shouting at Skittles. Before Odilon could figure out what to do, the man stabbed Skittles and took something out of his pocket before taking off down the street.

The Circle K cashier ran out the store shouting Skittles' name and Odilon joined him. There was blood on the tire pressure machine, and Skittles was breathing hard—he took Odilon's hand and pulled him in, saying "Save them. You got to save them." The cashier was on the phone calling for an ambulance, and all Odilon could do was tell Skittles that everything was going to be okay.

"Do you remember me, Skittles? Do you remember me? We talked at The Cafe one night—the Pelicans were playing the Bucks. Do you remember that night, Skittles?"

Skittles was breathing hard—he managed a smile.

"I remember," he said. "You are a nice young man."

His hand was covering his stab wound, and Odilon pressed his hand on top of his, hoping to stop the bleeding or at least to slow it down.

"Everything is going to be okay, Skittles. In good enough time, you'll be right back out here, and I'll fix you a nice drink at The Cafe. It'll be on me, Skittles—just hang on in there."

"You got to save them," Skittles said.

"Hang in there—everything is going to be okay."

It wasn't. He died. The puncture wound was too deep. Odilon watched the news during his shift at work that night. He had been trying his best to stay focused, but the morning had completely consumed him, and when he saw the report, he couldn't hide his tears. He kept thinking about what Skittles had said and mouthed his words over and over again.

"You got to save them."

The blood was still there on the tire pressure machine when Odilon was finally able to go back to the store—he got his cup of coffee and mini-pack of Oreos, and there were three men at the register talking with the cashier, Rousseau, the one who would shake his head and say, "There goes that Skittles—at it again every day" and laugh.

One of the guys said, "Another bet gone bad."

This made the cashier mad, and he shook his head.

"Mind your own—you have no clue."

"That was all it was—nothing else."

"Mind your own."

Odilon looked outside, and it was another pretty day, sunny—just like the day when Skittles died. The three guys left and Rousseau looked at him, shaking his head again.

"They don't know. They just don't know."

"What was it about?"

Rousseau leaned down behind the counter and took out a handful of items such as Snickers, SweeTarts, Tylenol, Zapp's Potato Chips, and chocolate chip cookies.

"That's all it was," Rousseau said.

He laughed and scratched his chin.

"The goods—just to keep the people going. All he wanted to do was give a bit of light to these people and for the kids. It was just for them to get by, that's all."

"Skittles," Odilon said.

"Skittles."

"Did they ever figure out about the guy with the knife? Was it about gambling like those guys just said?"

He fiddled around with his pack of Oreos. Rousseau shook his head.

"Nothing like that," Rousseau said. "He's a betting man—that's right—but it wasn't anything like that. He gave all that gambling cash to the people."

"Skittles," Odilon said.

"The man—that man who stabbed and killed Skittles there—that man was no good. He'd come in here asking for money for this and that and free things and all. I'm sure he was asking Skittles the same, and he wouldn't give it to him. He wouldn't give it to him because he knew that wasn't his calling. His calling was to help the people—not to give in to their own self-harm."

Odilon thought about all the times he'd approach strangers and ask for money or cigarettes, alcohol, or drugs.

"See," Rousseau said. "Skittles was the priest of the streets. He was showing love to the people who needed love, even if it was a little bit."

He slammed the counter with the palm of his hand.

"And Skittles wanted to help that man—that man with the knife. He told him he'd help him, but that man didn't want any help. And that's all Skittles could do—staying true to his words. The priest of the streets."

Odilon pushed his Oreos and coffee toward Rousseau while he rang them up.

Rousseau continued to shake his head.

"Those people—they're going to miss him. I'm going to miss him. Always making us laugh. Always making us see the light, even if it was just for a little bit."

Odilon thought about his last words to him, about saving them—about how he had to save them, and he mouthed his words over and over again. He thought about Ma and his dad and all the people he had hurt. He thought about all of the second chances he was given in life.

"I'll see you next time," Odilon said.

"Alright—you keep doing your thing. Skittles asked about you from time to time, you know."

Odilon stopped walking and turned around.

"What do you mean?"

He switched his coffee from one hand to the other.

"He knew your story—he did. He knew everyone's story around here. That's why he visited you. He saw something in you."

Odilon looked down, trying to understand what Rousseau was saying.

How did he know me, he asked himself.

"He saw you on the street a few times back then," Rousseau said. "He was telling me how you asked him for money or something like that and how you looked real bad off."

"What did he do?" Odilon asked, trying to remember.

"He helped you out."

"Why? He knew I was up to no good, right?"

"He saw the light in your eyes—he did," Rousseau said. "He was so happy that he saw you coming here and getting your cookies and coffee. He was happy that he was right—that your light came through."

"Damn," Odilon said.

He realized that Skittles came to The Cafe just to check up on him.

"Skittles," Rousseau said.

He laughed and shook his head.

"There goes that Skittles."

Still stunned, Odilon managed a smile and said bye.

Odilon didn't get into his car though—he put his Oreos and coffee on top of the tire pressure machine and lit a cigarette. I have some time, he thought, and leaned against the machine. And he waited there—he waited to see if anyone would come, and if they did, he'd give them his Oreos. He waited, thinking about the redfish Ma had cooked for him, and so they arrived, and they arrived with vague smiles on their faces.

Galileo's World

GALILEO TOLD the referee to fuck off and received her second technical foul in the middle of the first quarter—at the age of seven, she had already built herself quite a reputation with the league and its players, coaches, and parents. Her tantrums were pure and raw and passionate—she was a horrible player, averaging more technical fouls and turnovers than minutes, points, assists, and rebounds combined.

"One more time, G, and we'll have to ask you to leave the team," Coach said.

"But I love basketball," Galileo said.

"But you have to learn how to respect the game—the refs—your teammates."

"I love the players and the game, but Coach, those refs fuckin' sucked."

"I know," Coach said. "I mean, that's beside the point. You have to learn to play through it. It's the game of life, G."

"What's life without basketball, Coach?"

"I hope you never find out," he replied.

Two days later, Galileo entered the game with one minute left in the fourth quarter, and she told the refs that they fuckin' sucked, and she was kicked out of the game—ranting and screaming, she walked to the bench, flipping off one of the refs before sitting down. The crowd shouted at her, making Galileo stand up and raise her hands, asking for more. Soon, popcorn was thrown, and the game had to be stopped for fifteen minutes as the audience was asked to calm down and be respectful.

"Fuck y'all," Galileo said. "All of y'all."

After the game ended, Coach pulled Galileo aside.

"I'm sorry, G—but you can't be on the team anymore."

"What? Coach. Please, Coach—this is all I have."

"You're too much," Coach said. "It's too much. Work on your game and your temper and come back next season."

The coach gave Galileo a fist bump, and she was trying her best to keep the tears from coming down, looking away as she thanked the coach.

"Thanks for all that you do, Coach. I mean it."

"I appreciate that, G. I'll see you around—work on that game, and learn to respect the game."

"I got you, Coach."

Galileo left the Breaux Bridge gym and walked home—twenty minutes along Bayou Teche, still in her jersey, she started to feel cold as the sun was going down, and as the sun was going down, this was when she started to pick up her pace. The dark sky arrived quickly during the winter days—her least favorite season solely because of the walks home in the evenings. No one really bothered her—perhaps an occasional car driving by playing loud music and shouting would startle her from time to time, but there was one time, right after the second day of basketball practice, when a truck slowed down, and the driver started to curse at her. Galileo took a corner and ran down the street with tears, praying that the truck didn't follow her. Just in case, she jumped into a ditch and covered herself with leaves and branches, trying her best to slow her breathing. She hadn't seen that truck since then, but she was always looking around every time she walked home after that day.

As she was approaching her trailer, she sprinted. She always sprinted toward the end of her walk back home—at the stoop, she bent over, hands on her knees, and spat.

"Fuck," she said. "I got to get in shape."

She walked in—the screen door making its usual squeaks, barely hinged and working, and none of the lights were on. This was a ritual for Galileo—closing her eyes in the dark and tracing her fingers along the wall until she reached the switch.

"Boom," she said—the living room opened up to her.

This was her favorite part of the day, turning on the lights in each room. After that, she headed next door to Acre's place to pick up Galilei. Acre was outside in his rocking chair, going back and forth with Galilei in his lap—a small round table next to him with his coffee mug and ashtray.

"Hey, Mr. Acre." Galileo said. "What the fuck is up?"

"Now G," he replied. "You know you can't speak like that—Ma raised you better."

Galileo grazed her shoes against the dirt of the ground as Acre waved to a girl on a bike riding by—Galileo turned around and waved too.

"Oh I'm sorry, Mr. Acre," she said. "It just comes out, you know."

"Honey, I know. Now think about Galilei—all she's got is you and Ma. You got to raise her right. You and Ma—you know no one else can."

"I got fired today."

She scratched her head.

"I got kicked off the team today, Mr. Acre. Mr. Acre, I'm fucking done. I'm out. No more, Mr. Acre."

"You got to calm yourself down, little pea," he replied. "We all saw that coming, didn't we?"

"You're right about that," Galileo said. "I just get caught up. I love the game so much."

"Now make sure the game loves you," Acre said.

Galileo looked up at the sky and then at her little sister.

"Well she's got you, too," Galileo said. "We'd be lost without you, Mr. Acre. Fuck."

"Hush it with that language," Acre said. "Every day, every day."

Galileo walked up the stoop and Acre handed Galilei to her. A loud honking could be heard and once it stopped, a thick silence settled in before they both heard a rabbit scurry into the bushes that separated their properties. Galilei reached out and touched Galileo's nose, murmuring.

"My sweet sister," Galileo said, her voice lighter than usual.

She ran her fingers across her bald head.

"I'm here now," she whispered.

"Get back in now," Acre said. "I'll be out here for a little while if you need anything—Ma will be home later on tonight, she said. It might be a late night, G, so you take care."

Galileo nodded and walked back over to her trailer, gently swaying Galilei. She put her in the carriage on the dining table and tucked her in, kissing her sister on the head.

"What the fuck do we have here?" Galileo said, opening the fridge.

She pulled out some leftover boudin from Poche's Market, wrapped in brown paper, and put it on a paper plate that she had used the night before, still on the dinner table.

"Hold on," she said. "I'm coming, little sister."

Galileo was starving—the last time she'd eaten was a bowl of cereal in the morning. Her stomach rumbled, and she licked her lips looking at the wrapped boudin. She took out a bottle of baby formula and shut the fridge door, then started to feed Galilei, who sucked on the bottle with eyes wide open.

"There you go," Galileo said. "You got to get big if you're going to play basketball. Bigger than me. You got to be better than me. I'm no fucking good, sister. But you—I can see it, Galilei. I can see it in you—the universe is yours."

Galilei finished the bottle and Galileo rinsed it out. Before warming up the boudin in the microwave, she checked to make sure there was another bottle in the fridge.

"I'm hungry, sister," she said.

The microwave rattled. Galilei had already fallen asleep, which made Galileo smile.

"Keep dreaming," she said.

Taking the plate of boudin over to the living room, she turned on the TV, flipping the channel to ESPN—the Pelicans were playing the Cavs, and it didn't take Galileo too long to lose interest.

"Not tonight, Pels," she said. "Let's take a trip back to the glory days."

The boudin swished around in her mouth as she pressed *Play* on the VCR—a recording of the 1998 NBA Finals, the one where Michael Jordan hit the game-winning shot, his last shot. Galileo fast-forwarded to the last few minutes of the game and watched Jordan.

"That fucking footwork," Galileo said. "It's all in the fucking footwork."

She took the last bite of the boudin—seeing the empty plate, she looked at the dinner table, where there was one more link left. A bell rang from outside—a bicycle riding by.

"Tomorrow," she said, thinking that Ma might not have time to make any food.

There was always cereal, but it served as back-up to an empty fridge. The last few minutes of the game continued to play as she cleaned the table and put the remaining link of boudin back in the fridge. She rocked Galilei, who was still asleep, before sitting back down on the couch, rewinding and playing the Bulls game until she fell asleep.

Galileo woke up in her bed the next morning, and after realizing that she was in her room, her eyes sparkled, immediately recognizing that her aunt was home.

"Ma," she shouted as she rushed out of bed and sprinted to the living room, almost knocking over a chair.

"You're home, Ma."

She scratched her stomach and looked at Galilei, who was in her crib next to the sofa.

Ma kissed her on the forehead.

"Oh you're rocking the room, little pea," she said, parting Galileo's hair.

"I missed you, Ma."

"I know, little pea."

Galileo hugged her leg.

"I heard you had some trouble yesterday now, didn't you?"

"Mr. Acre told you?"

"Coach called."

"Coach called on a Saturday morning?"

"You know he really cares for you, G."

"I got fired, Ma."

"Now child, why do you behave like that? Did I raise you like that? Did I fail?"

Ma's voice was soothing, soft—Galileo felt bad knowing that she had let her down. She wasn't going to tell her that she was kicked off the team. Instead, she was going to say that she retired from the game because of a back injury.

Galileo watched her fix a bowl of cereal and put it on the dinner table for her—she realized that her aunt hadn't changed yet.

"You have it, Ma."

"I'm fine, little pea—I ate something on the way home. I'll head over to the store to pick up some lunch and dinner."

"Can you get some cracklin?"

"Now when do I never pick up any cracklin?" Ma said.

Galileo gave her a thumbs up and started eating her Fruity Pebbles.

"You need to apologize to Coach, to the team, and to the parents."

Galileo pushed her cereal away.

"You've got to learn now before it's too late," Ma continued.

"Too late for what?"

"Let's not find out now."

"I'm just trying to do right to the team, Ma. They're not on my level. They don't know how to compete, Ma. Did you know that Jordan didn't make varsity when he tried out? He had to play JV. Now he's the best player in the world. Best athlete. Six rings. Scoring. Defense. He had it all."

"He worked hard—he sure did," Ma replied.

"I'm working hard, too," Galileo said.

She watched the color of the cereal flakes turn the milk red.

"I know, G—keep working hard, but not just at the game, but with yourself. Now finish your cereal and wash up."

"Can I go to the park?"

"I'll take you down in just a bit before I go to the store."

"I think I smelled some crawfish in the air yesterday, Ma."

"It's coming," Ma said, patting Galileo on the back.

"5 pounds, two corns, and sausage—I can't wait."

She hugged her aunt and went to her room, where on her bed, she drafted words in her head about her apology.

"Fuck," she said.

The sun was bright that Saturday morning—in a chilled air, Galileo sat at a picnic table and watched a game at the park. She recognized some of them—others, she had never seen before, and she cheered on the ones she knew. They were all teenagers.

"Move your hands," she said to one of the players—Crete. "Move your hands and your feet. Fuck."

After the game, Crete walked over to Galileo, holding a basketball.

"I heard you got kicked off the team," he said.

"No I didn't," Galileo replied.

"Yes, ma'am—you sure did. My sister told me."

"She doesn't know anything."

"She knows she has playing time," Crete said.

He dribbled the ball between his legs and laughed.

"And you don't," he continued. "Not anymore."

"Fuck all of them," Galileo said.

Crete stopped dribbling.

"You're too young to talk like that. You got to back up your game before you start talking like that."

Galileo thought about Jordan and all the times she saw him trash talking during the games.

"Knicks," she mouthed to herself.

"And Ma lost her job, didn't she?" Crete added.

"What? No she fucking didn't."

"Yes, ma'am," he replied.

He paced in circles, looking at the concrete and dribbling the basketball a few times. Its sound echoed—amplified in Galileo's head. Her frustration with Crete scrunched her face, wanting to scream and shout.

"Shut the fuck up."

"Yes, ma'am. I heard it this morning—everyone knows. You didn't know?"

"I didn't know because it's not true."

"It's true."

"You're a fucking liar," Galileo said.

She thought about when she was talking to Ma earlier that day and how her aunt hadn't changed her clothes. Crete's figure became a blur as the sun was behind him—Galileo squinted and looked up into the sky, which was bare and blue. She felt cold.

"You don't know?" Crete said again.

A cardinal landed on the picnic table, briefly—it hopped around before taking off. Galileo felt hungry, and she started to think about boiled crawfish and potatoes and sweating as she peeled each tail. She loved the spice.

"They said that one of the employees was stealing money."

"Ma didn't steal any money—that's for sure."

"You're right—she didn't."

"You're just a fucking liar."

"Listen to me now," Crete said.

He bounced the ball hard with two hands. Galileo saw a couple walking a dog around the basketball court—she was trying to stay distracted.

"Ma knew who was stealing the money."

"So."

"So—she wouldn't tell."

"Good."

"Not good."

A Coke can rattled against the leg of the metal table as the wind blew. Galileo thought about boiled crawfish, and she wondered if Ma was going to bring back some cracklin.

"Because she wouldn't say," Crete continued, "they let her go."

"Mr. Ernie wouldn't do that," Galileo said. "Mr. Ernie is one of the good ones."

"It wasn't up to him—they said that the call came from office headquarters over in Mississippi—she came in herself and told them to their faces. Mr. Ernie lost his job and some say it was him who was stealing money."

"Fuck that," Galileo said.

"They say she's staying at Maison Madeleine—living it big while she's letting everyone go."

One of the players in the distance called out Crete's name.

Crete smiled—"Take it easy, G. Work on that game and work on your mouth. But definitely work on that game."

He trotted off, gently dribbling the basketball. Galileo shouted his name.

"Can I have your basketball?"

Without hesitation, he made a long pass to her—Galileo stood and fumbled the ball while trying to catch it.

"Meet the pass," Crete shouted, before joining his friend and walking off.

Galileo picked up the basketball and bounced it—its rhythm put her in a trance as she tried to make sense of what Crete had just said. The rattling of the Coke can became louder, and she kicked it.

"No fucking way," she said. "Ma. No way."

The court was empty, and Galileo jogged to one of the hoops and shot the ball—it barely reached the bottom of the chained net. She let the ball roll away into the grass behind the goal and sat right at the free throw line.

"What did you do, Mr. Ernie? What did you do?"

A honk took her out of her daze, and she saw Ma pulling into the parking lot—grabbing the basketball, Galileo ran over to the car and got in the back seat, next to Galilei who was tucked away in her carriage.

"Hey, Galilei," she whispered.

Ma backed out—"I picked up some cracklin, little pea."

"Thanks."

Galileo patted Galilei on the head and watched the couple walk away with their dog.

"What's wrong?"

"Just hungry."

Quiet for the rest of the ride, they pulled up to the trailer. Ma and Galileo started to unpack the groceries.

"Should I feed Galilei?" Galileo asked.

"I got it, little pea—have your cracklin."

They sat at the dinner table.

"There's a game tomorrow at the gym," Ma said.

Galileo opened up the cracklin and offered one to Ma—she took a piece.

"We're going to drop by so you can give your apologies."

Galileo squirmed in her chair—her breathing became loud, pushing the cracklin aside. She hadn't eaten any yet.

"I don't want to—I don't want to. Please. Please, Ma."

"It needs to be done—it's for your future. It's for the person you'll become."

"What about your future?" Galileo asked.

Ma stopped chewing, and she took the bottle out of Galilei's mouth and set it on the table, gently rocking the carriage.

"What do you mean?"

Galileo thought about Galilei and how she was always quiet—how seldom she cried, how she just looked around with big round eyes, observing the world. Why can't we all just be quiet like her, she thought.

"What do you mean by that?" Ma asked again.

Galileo pulled the cracklin closer to her, fiddling with the wrapping.

"Why didn't you tell them who stole the money?"

Ma could only assume she found out talking to someone at the park.

"I was going to tell you," Ma said.

She picked up the bottle and started to feed Galilei again.

"It's not so simple—the answer."

"So we won't have any money," Galileo said. "So we can't have food or light or food. What about Galilei? Will we have to move?"

Ma spoke in her low soothing voice—no matter what she would've said, it would feel calming and reassuring.

"Was it Mr. Ernie?" Galileo asked. "Say something—you told me never to lie. Don't lie, Ma."

"One," Ma said gently. "We will be okay. Don't worry. I'll take care of you and Galilei and us. We're staying right here now—that cracklin will still be on the table, and the lights will still be on."

Galileo needed to hear those words—she was trying her best not to cry.

"Two," Ma continued. "Yes little pea, it was Mr. Ernie."

Tears came down Galileo's face—she remained silent—they were silent tears.

"Three," Ma said.

She went on to explain why she didn't tell them. Their street was loud—children playing in the yards, traffic going through, shouting and laughing. Ringing bicycles. The smell of barbecue grilling was as loud as the families who were joking around on the stoops of their homes. It was a perfect day to be outside, and the day belonged to the neighbors.

Ma didn't reveal that Mr. Ernie was the one who was stealing money because he had helped many people, including them, whether it was financially or otherwise, and that the reason why he was stealing was because he was trying to support someone in need.

"It wasn't for himself," Ma said.

"I don't care about that," Galileo said. "I care about you. And me. And us."

"I know. I get it."

"How the fuck do you expect me to apologize and grow and all that if you can't tell the truth and lose your job?"

"One," Ma said. "Think about your father—my brother—when you speak like that and how he'd react if he heard you. How you'd hurt his feelings cursing and swearing, at his own sister, too."

She remained calm—never raising her voice.

"Two," she continued. "If you respect me—if you respect yourself, if you respect this baby here—you wouldn't talk like that. Hear me?"

"I hear you, Ma. Sorry."

Ma explained to Galileo that she had to make a decision—"I don't know if I made the right decision, I don't, but I just couldn't say it. He's done so much for everyone—literally everyone you know, G."

"Mr. Acre?"

"Including Mr. Acre."

Ma mentioned that she already has two strong leads to a new receptionist position.

"Mr. Ernie is still looking out for us—it's his sister's business. See. We're going to be okay."

Galilei reached out her hands, and Galileo took them, waving them up and down playfully.

"What about Mr. Ernie?"

"Him, too. Everyone in town knows him and what he's done. He'll be just fine."

That night, Galileo couldn't sleep—she shifted side to side, scrunched her pillow, adjusted the blanket, but no matter how much she tried, she couldn't relax.

"Fuck," she whispered.

She didn't change—pulling a small box out from under her bed, she snuck out through the window of her room, knowing that if she went through the front, Ma would hear the squeaking and rattling door. This wasn't the first time Galileo had snuck out through the window, but it was the first time doing so this late into the night. She walked over to Acre's place and looked at his bicycle, which he always kept outside, unchained. He kept it there in case someone needed it—a few times his previous bicycles had been stolen, but whenever he would get a new one, he'd never lock it or keep it inside—he wanted people to use it.

Galileo looked at Acre's bicycle—her impromptu plan already had a challenge, realizing that the bicycle was too large for her. She took it anyway, putting the box in the front basket—she couldn't use the seat, but instead, she pushed her body ahead of it, so that she could crouch down and pedal. Though the handlebars were in her line of vision, it was better than nothing, she thought—it's fucking dark, anyway.

"I promise I'll bring it right back, Mr. Acre," she said.

It had been awhile since Galileo visited Mr. Ernie with Ma, but she knew the general direction and headed that way, hoping she'd recognize buildings and street names. She remembered that it was one turn into a neighborhood—she just couldn't remember how far down the road, how many four-ways to cross, and if it was a left or a right turn. She rode the bicycle—wobbly and slowly—but it was moving, and she felt the cold air press against her nose, her watery eyes, but she was determined. It didn't take too long, though, for her to realize that she had become lost, not recognizing any of her surroundings, and acknowledging that perhaps she had ridden too far down the road to an area she had never been before.

"Fuck," she said, slowing down the bicycle, slightly stumbling as she came to a stop.

She turned behind her.

"Fuck. What the fuck, Galileo."

The silence of the city settled in, and it became overwhelming, making her feel scared and lonely. She thought about boiled crawfish, corn, and potatoes—the cracklin and boudin—and she focused on the red of the crawfish, full of spice.

Just ahead, she could see the flickering light of a gas station—a car drove by with its window down. It came to a soft roll as it passed Galileo— she looked at the driver and noticed the bright white teeth in the dark. That was all she could see. Everything else was fear.

"Galilei," she whispered, picturing her sister and herself eating at a restaurant.

"Little girl," the voice said, echoing in Galileo's head. "Little girl, it's too late for you to be out here right now. Where you going on that bike?"

All Galileo could see was the white of the teeth. The car's engine wasn't smooth, jerking and popping at times. Galileo thought about crawfish. She looked around.

"Little girl. Can I have that bike?"

That was all Galileo needed to hear for her to take off—she threw the bicycle down, stumbling over and falling, but she jumped right back up and took off into the darkness, taking a turn and stopping between two houses. She heard the car door squeak open—there was a sound of the bicycle dragging against the road, and then a loud slam. She looked around and saw that the fences on each side could be climbed, and she got her footing ready, still not feeling the pain in her legs from scraping them against the road. A perk in the engine, and she listened to it fade away—letting go of her breath, her chest heaved as the cold air rushed in.

Once the silence settled in again, Galileo cried.

She cried and she cried, letting it all out, not caring if anyone heard her. Barking could be heard, and it didn't take too long for the lights to come on in one of the houses next to her. Galileo walked out of the darkness and sat down on the edging of the wooden porch. She bellowed, and the door opened. She bellowed and felt a comforting hand on her shoulder. She bellowed and heard a familiar voice.

"It's okay, G. It's okay. I'm right here. It's okay. Are you hurt?"

Galileo turned her head around and through her tears, she saw Mr. Ernie, and as she recognized his face, she took in deep breaths to calm herself down and tucked in her head against his legs.

"I'm good," she managed to say.

Mr. Ernie picked her up and took her into the living room—its scent, the potpourri of the house, soothed Galileo as she sat on the couch and Mr. Ernie cleaned her legs, which were bleeding—cuts from the road. He asked her what happened, and she stuttered as she spoke, saying how she was riding her bike to his house so that she could give him some money.

"But the man took my bike," Galileo said. "I was too scared and I ran off, and the man took my bike and my money."

She started to cry again, and Mr. Ernie consoled her.

"Why were you trying to give me money?" he eventually asked.

"Because you were always helping people out and I heard you lost your job and I wanted to help you out."

"Oh dear," Mr. Ernie said. "Oh little pea."

He called Ma and Galileo fell asleep on the couch—when she arrived, she was clearly distraught—eyes red from crying, her clothes barely on her body, she stammered as she sprinted to her with Galilei in one arm and pushed Galileo's head against her chest, waking Galileo up. Ma spoke on in a soothing voice, rubbing her back. Mr. Ernie explained to Ma what had happened, and she thanked him over and over again.

"I'll see you soon, friend," Ma said as they walked out the door.

Ma drove back to the trailer while Galileo slept the whole time—not waking up as Ma held her and Galilei in each arm and put each of them to bed.

When Galileo's eyes opened the next morning, she saw Ma already sitting on her bed. She probably sat there the whole time, Galileo thought as she folded herself over and hugged her.

"I'm sorry, Ma."

"I know, little pea."

"I was just trying to help, Ma."

"I'm proud of you, little pea."

"I lost Mr. Acre's bike and my fourteen dollars."

"We'll get Mr. Acre a new bike—a better one, too, little pea. And you can get your fourteen dollars back easy with finishing some chores around the house, okay, little pea?"

"I love you, Ma."

"I love you, G."

"Ma."

"Yes, little pea."

"Can we get some crawfish today?"

"We sure can, little pea—after we go by the gym this evening, we'll get some dinner after."

"I hear you, Ma."

At the gym, Galileo was nervous—she had mouthed the apology over and over all day, but she would forget it every time, and now that she was in front of everyone, she froze even more. Coach was standing next to her—Ma sat in the stands, and the game clock was set at six minutes, getting ready for the first quarter.

"Everyone, please," Coach shouted and the crowd hushed. "Please give your attention to Galileo here—she has something to say."

A few groans could be heard, which made Ma laugh. Galileo motioned to Coach to crouch down.

"I'm sorry, Coach," she whispered into his ear. "I'm really sorry."

Coach patted her on the back.

"You're on the right path, G," he whispered back. "Be strong. Be brave."

"Fans of the game," Galileo shouted, standing straight with her head lifted. "I apologize for my behavior."

She looked over to the bench.

"I apologize to my teammates," she continued. "I am working on my behavior and my game, and I hope to one day return in full force. I apologize to y'all, big time."

Galileo bowed. The crowd stood up and applauded, and Galileo couldn't help but to smile and wave, feeling like a princess. After giving every one of her teammates a high five, Coach asked her if she was ready to return.

"Not yet, Coach. I've been thinking—how about this—how about next week, I come back and I'll be your assistant coach."

"Assistant coach?"

"I'll learn to love and respect the game, Coach, and the game will learn to love me."

"Deal," Coach said.

Ma, Galilei, and Galileo didn't stay to watch the game though—they walked out the gym, toward the car, and the evening sun shone behind them, providing solace. Its descent felt slower than usual to Galileo, and she closed her eyes and listened to the world around her.

"Mr. Acre will be meeting us there," Ma said.

"Where?"

"Where do you think?"

"Crawfish?" Galileo replied. "At Crazy Bout Crawfish?"

She had completely forgotten about it.

"You fucking know it," Ma replied.

The gleam in Galileo's face—the white of her teeth as bright as ever, and her smile lifted in sunlight, a laugh to remember. She grabbed Ma's hand and looked out ahead where she saw a cardinal in the sky, red and red—on its path, giving direction to Galileo's universe.

The Song of the Bark

THERE WERE no squirrels or egrets around when Fabienne and Foulon were taken by Lake Martin—so Verot had thought—perhaps there was one alligator, lazily wading that morning with one eye closed, which entered his mind just for a moment, but that was just a local rumor he had created in his own head, on that day of a certain spectacle of snow and ice causing such troubles for a city accustomed to the thickness of the sun. One day, it lasted. One day, all was gone for Verot.

Estranged since their birth, a rekindled relationship with his younger siblings eight months before a Louisiana blizzard. The twins welcomed their older brother, not knowing much—the parents didn't talk too much about Verot, thinking that he had given up on them. It's not so much that Verot had given up on them, but more so that he had lost his senses—living in a distorted reality where he had no family, just himself in a lonely world.

"We're losing him, Alcindor," Darbonne said. "Our son. We're losing him, and I don't know what to do. I am his mother, Alcindor."

Their parents—Alcindor and Darbonne—tried their best to keep the family together, but realizing that Verot had wandered into a maze in his own mind, much like the trodden paths of the sugar cane fields near their home, they decided to start fresh, and so came Fabienne and Foulon, even though Verot was still around at the time—but soon after, he became a ghost of a memory. No one knew where he had gone. Local talk—the whispers loud enough for Darbonne and Alcindor to hear—prated about his demise and possible location. Whether it was at the Chevron or Don's Seafood Hut or at the ArtWalk down Jefferson Street on Saturday nights, there was always talk, and with each turn of the tongue, Verot's mother felt the pain of losing the soul of her son.

"Please be kind," Darbonne said, walking into the lobby of La Fonda one Friday night after Verot had left.

It was their first time going out to dine since Verot's departure eight or so months earlier. Every now and then, a talk on the phone, or going to the grocery store at awkward hours, the drive-thru, yoga at home—they had lived a muted life, knowing that the town was talking about them—friends and strangers alike. Alcindor would arrive at his office early in the morning—around 4 a.m., just so that he wouldn't see anyone, and then he would leave late, after everyone had gone, and in between, quietly eating a sandwich at his desk. The only solace he found was talking to his clients who had no idea what he and his family were going through—relying on voices from around the world for a sense of belonging.

She knew people had been talking about them—her family, her son, though it had been almost a year—Lafayette gossip might have thinned out from time to time, but it never snapped, and entering her own little world again, she realized, would thicken the talk again. She knew because she would have been doing the same if it wasn't about her own family. The room was full of echoes—little space to navigate around, chatter and chatter. Frozen margaritas lifted in the air so that they didn't spill against shuffled bodies. Alcindor didn't want to attend. He knew what they would be walking into—thinking about all of the times he fueled the Lafayette gossip, whether true or otherwise. He knew better not to, and it wasn't like he enjoyed it—he only took part in the conversation to reaffirm his companionship, to be a part of something, to fit in.

"Let's stay home, Darb—there's no need for this."

"There is a need," she replied. "We might as well get it over with anyway, and it's our time to eat the burnt crust of the pan. We deserve it."

When they pulled into the parking lot, they both sat in their Mercedes for eleven minutes, engine running. Darbonne had gotten out of the car before Alcindor, walking into the restaurant by herself, while Alcindor listened to the traffic on Johnston Street.

Her friends, both casual and closer, welcomed her—hugs, pats, kisses on the cheeks. Darbonne felt the betrayal and judgment—the façades and fronts with each person she met.

"Please be kind," she said again.

That was all she could say, over and over, before finding a spot in the corner of the room, pulling out her phone and pretending to use it. Soon enough Alcindor entered, also pretending to talk on the phone. He smiled and waved and laughed and nodded his head, as if he was having the most jovial conversation. They patted his back as he made his way and eventually found Darbonne, who was trying her best to keep her composure. They all stood and stared at them. Alcindor, usually quiet and peaceful in demeanor, even when faced with confrontational situations, couldn't take it anymore.

"Stop," he shouted. "Stop looking at us."

This, of course, had caused the restaurant to hush, but only briefly, and the crowd went on about their business as Darbonne and Alcindor contemplated their existence in such a tiny world.

"Should we move?" Alcindor asked, later on that night, at home.

"What would that fix? The gossip, the talk—it'll all still be there, whether we're here or not."

She watched the sitter, a childhood friend of Verot, drive off while she cradled the newborns, their eyes closed. Alcindor had ventured off into his own dreams of a time when life was good, his own eyes closed as he stood outside on the back patio—a large oak before him. He opened his eyes—traces of the bark defined under the porch light. A shovel neatly tucked into the dirt, just a bit away from the garden, where he and Verot had buried their dog, Petite, a Catahoula which the family took in as a puppy—stray and gentle, Petite became the stronghold for them. Not only was it the last time that Alcindor saw Petite, but it was also the last time he saw his son before he took off into his own labyrinth, to return years later.

"She did real good, right, Dad?" Verot said, panting as he opened the dirt for Petite.

"Real good, son," Alcindor replied.

"A real good pup, right, Dad?"

"A real good pup, son."

The tears came down—Verot didn't wipe his face. It had been awhile since he had last cried, and the release felt refreshing. He put his head on Alcindor's shoulder, heaving into the cloth of his shirt. He dug his face into the collar of his father's neck.

"I'm real sorry, Dad," Verot said, his voice muffled.

"What's wrong, son? Why are you sorry? What's wrong, son?"

"I know I'm not Petite."

Alcindor wrapped his arm around Verot and pulled him in tight.

"I know I'm not the son you hoped for," he stuttered, taking in deep breaths. "I'm a real mess-up."

"You're no mess, son," Alcindor replied, himself trying not to cry. The pain he felt in his son's voice, knowing that he had done nothing wrong—knowing that his son's anguish was far gone from any consolation he could provide.

"I'm so wrong," Verot said.

He lifted his head and looked into his father's eyes. Alcindor couldn't get himself to look at Verot—not because he was ashamed or embarrassed, but because he knew if he did, he would break down as well. He looked at the oak and its bark, thinking how this tree had seen so much and how it knew the family more than the family knew itself. Just next to them lay Petite wrapped in her favorite blanket, a faded pink with the edges shredded and torn.

The crying entered silence, and Verot stared into Petite's grave. He pictured himself cuddling with Petite inside of it.

"Son," Alcindor said. "You've done no wrong, son. I love you."

"I love you."

Alcindor hadn't heard Verot say those words since he was a child.

"Let's get some help," he said, rubbing his son's back.

Verot nodded.

"It's time," he said.

A raccoon scurried over the fence as the sun came down—its twilight creating a frame of faded solace, one that neither of them knew the importance of in that moment together.

"I'm sorry," Verot whispered.

"Don't be, son."

They buried Petite, and the next morning, Verot was gone, leaving all of his belongings.

"It's time," Alcindor whispered to himself, over and over again that day, realizing what his son had meant.

"Alci," Darbonne said. "Alci. Alcindor."

She called out his name until he was taken out of the past. He wiped his eyes and turned around.

"I miss him."

Darbonne wrapped her arms around his waist.

"Every morning I walk into his room, just in case."

They stood on the back patio—the moon in puzzle pieces cut from the branches of the oak—and that was their night.

With the arrival of the twins, Darbonne and Alcindor enjoyed a fresh start to a new life, though they continued to be haunted by Verot's exit. Their children gave the parents a normal experience—the usual makings of a family with no worries other than those of scraped knees, tantrums, and running errands nonstop. They loved it. They became more accustomed to being a part of society again, and the whisperings about Verot had diminished, though sometimes they still reverberated in their ears on random nights when the children were out and they had the night to themselves. They kept the friend circle tighter this time around, but all in all, they had become the past again, a time before Verot had become lost—a time when Alcindor and Darbonne could turn around and not worry about who would be standing there.

Fabienne and Foulon loved to be outside—it was a remnant of Verot, who had done the same when he was at home. It could be pouring down with gusty winds, or it could be 100 degrees in a drenched air—there was no situation which kept the twins away from the outdoors. It was on such a day, one of a tropical storm, while they sat out on the porch swing and watched the rain come in sideways, they saw Verot walking down the street without a shirt. He wasn't in a rush—he walked as if he was strolling around Girard Park in mid-April. When Fabienne and Foulon saw him down the road, they rushed over—Fabienne took off her coat and gave it to him. She saw his smile in the rain—a smile that Verot gave, feeling kindred with the siblings.

"Come over to our house," Foulon shouted. "It's just down there."

He pointed behind himself, still facing Verot.

"Thank you," Verot quietly replied, as if they were in church.

Though Fabienne and Foulon wanted to run back to the house, they slowly walked with him under the thunder. Their parents were on the porch as they approached. Verot felt his mother's gasp as she fell to her knees. He heard his father's breath as he ran out in the rain.

"Home," Verot said.

It didn't take too long for Verot to become familiar with his younger siblings, who were all too welcoming, though it did take him some time to reacquaint himself with his surroundings again, including his parents. Darbonne and Alcindor were gentle and caring, almost still in disbelief that their son had returned.

"It's the family we never had," Alcindor said. "I just washed his clothes."

"I just fixed him a plate of spaghetti," Darbonne said.

That first day that Verot returned, the day of storms and chaos, he found his room to be exactly the same as it was before.

"It never changed," Verot said in a thin, fragile voice.

"Let's go see Petite," Alcindor said.

Where was he all this time?

Verot visited the Chitimacha Tribe and learned their ways, finding peace with himself and the world inside of him.

"We were worried," Darbonne said, "that—you know—"

"I know. I'm sorry."

"We're so happy you're back," Alcindor said. "I still look at you, and I still see you when you were as tall as my knees."

"I still am, Dad," Verot said.

He kissed his father on the cheek.

The moments Verot cherished the most were when he was with Fabienne and Foulon, particularly when they played outside together—whether it was throwing the ball around or reading a book out loud or just staring at the sky, Verot found himself overwhelmed with happiness—an uncertain feeling. Though he was their older brother, the twins saw him as an uncle of some sort, and they smothered him with love, reminding him of how he loved the Catahoula.

"I had to, Dad," Verot said one night—they stood in the backyard just as they had done the night he had departed.

"Fabienne and Foulon—I knew I couldn't be around them—I didn't want to ruin their worlds or show them the sadness and pain that I felt."

"We could've figured it out, son," Alcindor replied, "but I understand. We're just glad that you're here—that you're back."

"I love them, Dad."

"They love you."

"I did real good."

"You did real good, son."

A weary spectacle, indeed—that day Fabienne and Foulon were taken by Lake Martin. Lafayette Parish and its surrounding areas had shut down—icy roads, covered in snow and slush, a condition the Deep South only met as an erratic acquaintance. Verot sat out on the porch swing and watched a blackbird covered in snow fly and perch itself on a heavy branch. Fabienne and Foulon walked outside.

"Let's go," Verot said.

"Where?"

"Let's go," Verot said.

Verot had fond memories of visiting Lake Martin when he was a child—when he became lost in his own mind, those flashes of the lake were what helped him to return. All it took was a fishing pole, a book, and a cooler full of Hi-C, and the day was his to remember. Verot wanted to give the same memories to his beloved siblings.

They took Alcindor's F-150, and Verot drove slowly and the roads were still slick—there wasn't too much traffic out and about, and they listened to 89.3 on the radio while he told Fabienne and Foulon about his previous visits to the lake when he was a child.

"Those days were golden," Verot said, almost to himself more than to his siblings.

The drive, taking longer than usual, took about 45 minutes, and when they arrived at Lake Martin, it was bare—no one was there, and it all looked so gray to Verot.

"The woods have changed a bit," he whispered.

They all hopped out of the truck—Fabienne and Foulon grabbing the cooler, Verot the fishing poles—and they made their way to a bit of land which jutted out into the water.

"This was where I sat—every time."

He looked up at the white sun and breathed in the cold air.

"I'll be right back," he said. "I forgot the tackle box."

A quiet splash, indeed—so there was silence.

As it happened and so it went, when Verot returned from the truck, Fabienne and Foulon were gone. The air pricked his skin as his breath shortened, his eyes large. It was silent that day, and there were no egrets and squirrels to be seen.

A shout and an echo, and an echo and a shout.

Nothing.

Nothing at all for Verot.

And so the world blinded him as he fell to dirt.

It wasn't until the next morning when he woke up—Fabienne and Foulon had found him on his side, still holding the tackle box in one hand and the fishing pole in the other. The siblings, drenched and shivering, were more worried about their elder brother than finding warmth for themselves. They had picked him up—a sibling at each end of his body, as if they were ridding a death, and put him inside the truck. Now, neither Fabienne nor Foulon knew how to drive, but they had visited the Kart Ranch several times and used those experiences to guide them out of Lake Martin and onto the side of the highway.

Verot awoke—crying.

"Fabienne," he gasped. "Foulon."

Repeating their names only to feel the skin of his mother press against his face, a soothing voice.

"Sleep, dear."

Verot saw flashes of his siblings as he closed his eyes.

Just across the Grand 16—Judice Inn, the family was there eating a late lunch, double cheeseburgers all around, except for Verot who was snacking on a bag of Cajun Crawtator Zapp's. The bulk of the customers had already left as it was the late afternoon, and the restaurant was down to a quiet murmur. There was laughing and there was smiling—shoulders brushing against each other, loving taps and shoves. The whole family. They were there.

Verot had made much progress, being able to situate himself in reality more and more each day since the morning when he thought Fabienne and Foulon were gone. Finding coping mechanisms for the tricks of the mind, help sought for both him and his parents who wanted to learn how to support him. Of course, the twins were a whole new world of energy, making Verot realize that voices in his head were far less important than the voices from his younger siblings.

As they left Judice Inn—the twins with their parents, and Verot riding his bicycle down to Acadiana Comics—he went around to the back of the restaurant to take a quick look at the coulee. It was a shiny day. He peered over, leaning on the wire fence, and saw a figure not too far off, just at the tip of the concrete where it descended down to the stream.

He paced from one end to the other—it was a pretty day outside, and he moved quickly, back and forth as if he was in trouble but he couldn't do anything about it—as if he was tied down to a post. The sun shone down on him. Verot tilted his head in wonder.

He was mumbling and then shouting at times.

It was pretty outside that day.

He started to bark as he paced, keeping his head up, projecting his voice. Verot listened to him. He continued to bark until he started to cough, and then he spat. Exhausted, he lay flat on the concrete with his face up toward the sky. Above, the bright white clouds were moving fast, dizzying. He was losing his breath. Verot looked back around—his family had left. He felt—briefly—a cold thin air.

The man prompted himself up, legs crossed—hands hanging over his knees. He stood. He peered over from where he stood at the top of the banks, barking again. The ditch was deep. The sun shone. Cars drove by, and it was a pretty day outside. Verot climbed over the wire fence and heard, faintly, a kitten's song—a sad lullaby.

Verot leaned his head forward and tumbled over down into the coulee. And the barking stopped, only sounds of grunts before he reached the bottom, and there was silence. The cry of the kitten had stopped—after the silence, Verot walked along the concrete bank of the stream. He looked down and breathed in, feeling a muted world settle in—recognizing a friend in a stranger. There was Petite, a time ago. He knew what he saw, and he saw the kitten nestling itself against the neck of the man, licking his face as he smiled and gently barked, singing his own song, a song that Verot once chimed. It was a pretty day.

The Rock and the River

THEY BECAME the lies they wished they never told—the sharp red of the crawfish pressed against the Abbeville air and coming through the door, the Vermilion seeped in through the humidity, over creased and weathered wooden tables, each striation, a story never heard—a mere rock and a river in a universe speckled with stars and stillness.

No one would know that it wasn't just a chipped hut or a dim shack, wooden and unpolished from the outside, but just one step inside, a world compacted into cubes, full of cayenne and corn and onions, a layer of the atmosphere in itself. Just around the corner, the cooks drenched in spice and sweat played their own melodies of histories while the water boiled in volcanic fashion, drenching tails with seasoned minds. A graying Argentino—a lick for each paw—crouched near a dripping hose. Such eyes had seen so much, waiting for a royal dinner of andouille and crab cakes over peppered concrete.

Down the road, under two streetlights—barely existing, Shantanu and Michot stood in an unkempt field, puffs of green blades sprouting toward the dark. Three wickets tucked into the dirt as Shantanu held a bright yellow ball, explaining to his friend about the game of cricket and its rules.

"It's almost like a catapult," he said, whirling his hand. "You just kind of wind up and let it go."

He took a few steps and moved his arms like he was bowling, and Michot shadowed him.

"And you can hit the ball backward?" Michot asked.

Shantanu's teeth gave way under the light.

"That's wild," Michot said.

Shantanu handed him the ball.

"Give it a go."

Back inside, the ceiling fans rocked and swayed—a motion much like a crowd with arms around each other's shoulders, moving to the hypnotic sounds of Corey Ledet at the Festival International de Louisiane in late April. In the corner of the room, at a long table—for those bigger reservations—sat Shaq among a group of friends, his knees shuffling left and right as he leaned over, peeling shells. Not quite a regular, but it wasn't his first visit, and he had formed a cordial acquaintance with Sabine, who had been working there for three years while attending SLCC.

"What's it called again?" Shaq asked.

He leaned back as she refilled his glass of water.

"It's called 'The Love Song Of J. Alfred Prufrock,' and it's written by T.S. Eliot," Sabine said.

"How does that line go again?" Shaq asked.

Sabine emptied the plastic containers full of shells and tails.

"Do you need more horseradish?"

"Michelangelo," Shaq replied, looking at the remaining crawfish.

He wiped the sweat off his forehead and looked at the last of the corn, saving it for the end. It was his favorite part—dipping the cobs into the sauce which had already been through an endless number of tails, creating a mixture of a tangy spice, sprinkled with Cajun salt rubbed and fallen from heads and claws.

"That's one part of it," Sabine said, balancing empty plates. "But the line I was talking about was sawdust restaurants with oyster shells."

"And the faces," Shaq said.

"'There will be time, there will be time,'" she replied, "'to prepare a face to meet the faces that you meet.'"

Shaq nodded his head—trying not to rub his eyes, he kept his hands on the table.

"But what does it all mean, Sabine? What does it mean?"

"You'll have to come back next time and find out, won't you now," she said, patting his shoulder before walking away.

"Damn," Shaq said.

He picked up the corn and fiddled with it while the rest of his friends were talking, removed from the conversation.

"Marmalade," he mouthed, dipping the cob into the sauce.

He was lost in his thoughts and without realizing it, he rubbed his eyes—an act Shaq was trying to avoid all night—and soon came the burning tears, blinding his vision, squinching his face this way and that, causing his friends to laugh.

Outside—Shantanu and Michot were still working on cricket. Michot bowled the ball, trying to sync his legs with the motions of his arms, and his pitch would go everywhere it wasn't supposed to go, sometimes taking them lengthy minutes to search for the ball in the dark corners of the spiky field. Michot panted.

"It's not looking good, is it," he said.

"It takes practice," Shantanu said, tossing the bright yellow ball in his hand. "You'll get it."

Shantanu handed him the bat.

"Give this a go," he said. "Just try to focus on the ball and block it from hitting the wickets—protective practice."

Shantanu was gentle with his bowls, helping his friend go through the motions, and once Michot was able to tap the ball a few times, he was feeling good about himself.

"Next up, a sixer," he joked.

They took a break and sat on the road, Gatorades in hand—the buzz from the restaurant was so constant that it felt like silence to them. Michot looked up, counting every star he saw while Shantanu focused on an armadillo making its way through a ditch across from them. It was those quiet moments, in muted ways, that brought Shantanu and Michot closer together, more so than any conversation or dinner or any other activity that required some kind of talking. When they were silent, the world was silent, and that was all they needed.

Shantanu put his arm on Michot's shoulder and leaned his head against his friend's neck, like when they were children sitting in golden fields full of bales and tractors under a summer sun. It had been ten years since their friendship had ceased, only to be reunited over a funeral a year ago—Michot's grandfather who had raised him and his sister—Shantanu's only friends at the time were the siblings, and his fond memories of Chalmette led him to the service knowing that he served as a father to the two. This was the first time they met each other since the funeral—Michot had reached out to him just a week before.

"I'm glad we're friends again," Michot said, one eye closed while looking up at the stars.

"What even happened?" Shantanu asked. "I don't know why we stopped."

"It's my fault," Michot said. "I stopped it—it's my fault and I feel bad about it."

Shantanu picked up a pebble and skipped it against the road like it was a river.

"That brings back some memories," Michot said, watching the rock tumble over.

A piano could be heard in the distance, coming from one of the houses a block down.

"You went to college and I didn't," he added. "I felt like you were leaving me."

"I still didn't have any friends," Shantanu replied. "I still felt really alone, and I never heard from you. I needed you, you know."

"I'm sorry."

"I got into a lot of trouble, and I had no one."

Shantanu didn't realize how angry he felt until that point—finally being able to let out thoughts he had kept to himself for years.

"What kind of trouble?"

"All the bad things, pal—it wasn't looking good. Not at all."

"You good?"

"I think so—I'm surprised that I'm still alive, but I think so."

"It really meant a lot to see you at the service, you know that, right? You were the only person that made me smile when I saw you there. My sister, too. It meant a lot."

Shantanu picked up another pebble and skipped it, coming to a stop when it reached the grass on the other side.

"I want to lick those stars," Michot said.

"Yeah. I know."

"How are your folks?"

"They're good—they're good," Shantanu said, almost in a whisper. "They're good."

"What about your brother? Bipin?"

"He's doing well for himself—he really is, and I'm really proud of him, you know."

"Proud of your little brother," Michot said, nodding his head. "I know the feeling."

They each felt a hand on top of their heads—cigarette smoke in the air—Shantanu breathed it in.

"Hey, jerk," Michot said. "You done?"

Shantanu leaned his head back and looked at Michot's sister upside down as she dragged in her cigarette, its orange-tipped glow reminding him of fireflies.

"Done and done," she said, tapping Shantanu's forehead. "So good to see you."

Shantanu stuck out his tongue.

"Let's get," Michot said.

"Y'all want to go for a drive?" Shantanu said. "Baton Rouge—maybe we can sneak down to the Mississippi like when Mr. Chalmette would take us."

"I'll get the wickets," Michot said.

"The what?" Sabine replied.

"If you don't know, you don't," Michot said.

He took the cigarette from her mouth and puffed on it while he jogged off for the cricket gear.

"You're happy," Shantanu said. "I'm glad that you're happy, Sabine."

She hugged him.

"Damn. Last time I saw you was at our grandfather's funeral. I'm sorry we didn't get a chance to talk."

Shantanu patted her arm.

"Before that," Sabine continued, "fuck—I was like just up to your waist then."

"I haven't grown much since then—but you have, little sister."

"It feels nice to hear that again—to hear your voice."

They got into Shantanu's truck—the wickets and the bat were in its bed. Michot sat in the back while Sabine was in the front with Shantanu. She was telling them about Shaq and Prufrock—her voice full of excitement.

"He's a big tipper, too," Sabine said. "Like a really big tipper."

She pulled out her folded cash—thick.

"Let's hit Ruth's Chris," Shantanu said.

"On me," Sabine said. "What you think, Michot?"

"Potatoes au gratin," he replied. "That's all I got to say."

"Tomorrow night, folks," Sabine said.

She lit a cigarette and gave it to Shantanu.

"You want one, big brother?"

"I'll just take a drag of yours."

The wind flapped in fast—all the windows were down, and they listened to KRVS on the radio as Shantanu headed to the highway. At the lights, Shantanu felt his phone buzz, and he pulled it from his pocket to check it, but a loud banging came from the back of the truck, making all three of them jump in their seats. Shantanu looked in the rearview mirror and saw two men—one held the cricket bat, and the other held a wicket—they continued to bang the gear against the side of the truck.

"What do you want to do?" Shantanu asked, putting up the windows.

Michot looked behind him.

"I don't feel like it," Michot said. "Just run the red."

The oncoming traffic had a steady flow though—Shantanu didn't want to back into them, but he couldn't make a U-turn either without putting his friends in danger. The back of the window crashed in, and Michot ducked, feeling bits of glass on his neck.

"Fuck," Michot said.

"Get in the front," Sabine said.

He crawled over the center console and sat on the right side—Sabine was in the middle.

"Get down for a second," Shantanu said, motioning to Michot's sister. "I'm just so curious," he continued, looking at Michot.

Michot looked at his sister—the two men were on each side of the truck, banging on the windows. The lights turned green.

"Gun it," Michot said.

The truck screeched as Shantanu pressed hard on the accelerator.

"You good?" Michot said.

"I'm good, big brother," Sabine replied.

They drove down and pulled into a gas station just before the lane merged into the highway. The back of Michot's neck was covered in cuts—Sabine had a few nicks, too. Shantanu went inside to find whatever he could get to help his friends clean themselves up, and they sat on the bed of the truck.

"Damn," Shantanu said. "They have my bat. That bat meant so much to me."

"Sorry," Sabine said.

"Well," Michot added, "what a way to lose it, right?"

"You're right about that, pal."

They let the night settle in before deciding that they would go to the river on another day. On the way back to his friends' house—just before dropping them off—Shantanu looked at his phone and then put it back in his pocket.

"Tomorrow," Sabine said, "after we go to Ruth's Chris."

"You got it," Shantanu said, giving Michot and his sister high fives.

"We'll take my jeep this time," Michot said, grinning.

That next day—that very next day, Michot couldn't get in touch with Shantanu.

"Maybe he brought his truck to the shop, and he's just really busy," Sabine said.

"Maybe," Michot said, "but I just feel like something is wrong, you know?"

He called Shantanu's home number—a dialing he hadn't saved in his phone but rather one that was remembered from his childhood—impressed in his brain after pressing those buttons over and over again until it became an infinite memory. With each number he pressed, flashes of their youth diffused into his mind—shooting hoops, playing in the front yard, walking down the road and looking for bottles and aluminum cans, hide and seek, learning how to drive or how to smoke cigarettes next to the Walgreens—and an overwhelming feeling of nostalgia took over, one that caused him to think about the ways he had left him after high school. He thought about his grandfather cooking dinner for them on Saturday nights or the scent of saris belonging to Shantanu's mother when he went over to their house. The phone rang and no one picked up.

They waited all day, and it wasn't until five in the evening when he and his sister decided to drive over to Shantanu's home—one that Michot hadn't visited in years, but heading toward his house felt like going home. They turned onto Tolson Road from Verot, not too far from Comeaux High School—a route Michot hadn't taken since he had dropped off Shantanu at his house the morning after their graduation party—red eyes, hoarse voices, and messy hair. That was the last time they saw each other until the funeral service for Michot's grandfather ten years later.

"The grass is long," Sabine said as they pulled up to the driveway.

"I'll cut for them," Michot replied. "They used to have a gardener years ago, but I'm not sure what they do now."

As they walked up to the door, Michot felt like he was frozen in a photo taken years ago. Not much had changed except for the paint on the garage—now a dark blue, when it was once maroon. He rang the bell and knocked on the door, but there was nothing—just silence coming from inside.

"It just isn't right, sister," Michot said.

They heard barking coming from the backyard of the neighbor's house, and its front door opened. Sabine waved to an elderly man dressed like church, Cajun skinned.

"Do you know if they're home?" she asked.

"We're friends," Michot added. "We can't seem to get in touch with Shantanu or anyone else."

Michot noticed Shantanu's truck parked in front of the mailbox—its back window still smashed from the night before.

"He didn't bring it to the shop," Sabine said, also seeing the truck.

"Oh, he's gone," the neighbor said.

His voice was gentle.

"Gone?" Michot replied.

"He's gone," the elderly man said again. "They took him away last night—I know that."

"They?"

The man sat on the stoop of the porch, holding a book.

"Yeah," he continued. "They came and took him away."

The neighbor looked up at the sky to see a flock of birds making their way past a lowered sun—he squinted his eyes and nodded his head, whispering words to himself as if he was having a conversation with a ghost.

"Sorry," he said out loud.

"Who took him and where?" Sabine asked.

"The box did—they sure did."

The flock of birds had become sprinkles in the sky.

"They were here last night," he continued, "and then they took him away in the box, stretcher and all, they did."

"What about his parents—his family?" Michot asked.

"Oh, they've been gone, now, they've been gone."

"Gone," Michot repeated.

"Gone."

"His brother, too?"

Oh, he's gone too, now."

The elderly man nodded his head.

"They're all gone now."

Michot turned to his sister, speaking quietly.

"Maybe Lourdes," Michot said, "it's the nearest one."

"Let's go by," Sabine whispered, her voice wavering.

All she could think about was when she and Shantanu would visit, and how she would run up to him and tug on his shirt, asking for a hug.

"Thank you, sir," Michot said.

"If you find him," the man replied. "Tell him I'm taking good care of Raj—he's in good care with me, and I got him. He's good."

Michot looked at him, trying to make sense of what the neighbor was saying.

"That's him in the back," the Cajun-skinned man said. "Exploring the worlds between the blades of grass—I got him, and he's in good care. If you find him, you tell him."

"His dog," Sabine said.

Michot thanked him again—in the jeep, he put all the windows down, letting in the flapping wind and the sounds of traffic to help him think, concentrate, trying not to let the sinking feeling overtake his brain. There were quiet tears—from both of them.

Room 204. That was Shantanu's room. That was where they found him—drowsy but awake. The TV was on mute—the lights were on, bright—the curtains pulled to let in the Lafayette evening sun, a welcoming.

"I'm sorry," Michot said. "I'm so sorry."

He was on one side, and Sabine was on the other side, each holding Shantanu's hands.

"When did this happen?" Michot asked.

"Three years ago, yesterday," Shantanu replied, his throat trying to find strength.

"Where was the service? You know we would've been there—you know that, right?"

Michot wasn't sure if he was telling the truth, perhaps convincing himself more than his friend.

"I took them back to my mother's land," Shantanu replied. "It was the only way—the Ganges welcomed their ashes, a lotus flower for every year they all had lived."

He shifted his body slightly, toward the easing sunbeams.

"164. An infinity of petals floating away from my soul."

Michot couldn't hold it in—nor could his sister—the tears came. There was crying. There was sobbing. He pressed his cheek against Shantanu's forehead before kissing him on the cheek—his friend's face streaked with his own sorrows.

"And you?" Sabine managed to say, firmly grasping Shantanu's hand, though it trembled.

"I had so much fun last night—I did. It was so much fun, and I didn't know what to do when I got back home. I didn't know what to do, and it was so much fun. I just wanted to be with my parents—my brother. I didn't want to lose that feeling—to be happy. I tried, you know."

The evening news was on TV—still muted, but if they turned on the volume, they would've heard how Shaq was in town for a donation he made to Lafayette High School's sports facilities. He was being interviewed.

"It's like this poem 'Prufrock,'" he said.

Michot caressed Shantanu's hair. Sabine still held on to his hand.

"We're here," Michot said. "We're never leaving you. I'm so sorry. You're our family. I'm so sorry."

Shantanu lifted his arm—slowly—with the IV attached and patted Michot's shoulder. He pulled Sabine in close. A clip of Shaq on TV—holding a basketball while talking to the local reporter—the room was mute. The world was mute, and that was how they wanted it to be.

It was dark—night, and they were on the banks of the Mississippi River, not too far from Baton Rouge. They were all there—Michot, Sabine, and Shantanu, and Raj was there, too, resting in the mud. The engine of Michot's jeep sang its own song a bit away, headlights shining, and Nina Simone's "Sinnerman" oscillated through the air, softly reaching the three friends.

Sabine was on her back staring at the stars while Michot and Shantanu ran their fingers through the water. Michot whistled along, responding to the faint sounds of the music. Shantanu threw a rock into the river—Michot did the same, and they took turns, throwing rocks into the Mississippi.

"Are you ready for next week?" Shantanu said.

"Not at all," Michot said.

"It'll be fun."

"You can hit the ball backward, right?"

"Anywhere you want to—knock it anywhere."

"Anywhere?"

"Anywhere."

Sabine joined in.

"How about that gratin?" she said. "Like I promised—it's on me."

It was quite a night, that night—for the three of them, together on the banks of the Mississippi, feeling kindred—the water tying itself to a friendship. The potatoes au gratin, too, and it was all so spectacular, indeed. That next week, Shantanu took Michot and Sabine to the parking lot of Griffin Hall, on one of the edges of the University of Louisiana at Lafayette's main campus to play in a cricket match held monthly just outside the building. They were under the streetlights, bright, and Michot even got a hit. He didn't knock it behind him as he wished, but it was a hit, and the way it sounded—it sounded like throwing a rock into the river at night, only to vanish in the dark—only to last forever in the silent echoes of the Mississippi.

Opelousas Electric

BASIN WAS in the dryer—perched in the backyard on a sunshine day, just behind the clothesline, glittered with towels and bedsheets that created a colorful array of quilted ghosts, floating—peering through its opening with one hand covering the left half of his face, chin to forehead, he saw the world in slits through the refracted gleams of the glass door.

"If you turn your head this way and that, it looks like we're all tumbling," he said with a voice full of adventure—as if he was talking to a friend.

Calais walked out through the back of the house—the grass prickled her bare feet, making her tiptoe toward a patchy spot in the yard. She looked around while the sun was on her back—freckled shoulders in constellation—calling out his name as a dragonfly whirled around her head. The dryer rattled. Basin heard the faint sounds of music, head lifted like the ears of a pup, hearing those magical words.

"Ice cream," he whispered.

The dryer shook as if it was alive.

"Get you out of there, short sweet," Calais said.

"Dodo," Basin called out. "Dodo—Dodo—Dodo—Dodo."

Calais heard the distant music, too—a pillow for the air, so it seemed on that April evening in Opelousas.

Dodo. Dodo was the first word Basin started to mouth ten or so months after he had ventured into this tumbling world—this was when he was trying to call out for his father. Dada, but Dodo, and Dodo wasn't around anymore—gone—dead. Dodo remained though, as the name shifted over toward his mother, fingers pressed against her chin, feeling her nose or ears, tracing his fingers around her neck—Dodo, he would mouth, and Calais was his only universe.

"Get you out of there."

"Dodo—Dodo," Basin echoed.

"Now I know—I know, short sweet. You coming?"

The dryer shook. Basin, making the machine come alive, opened its mouth—he hopped out in one fluid motion and rolled toward his mother like a bent wheel. Then came a cartwheel.

"How long were you in there?" Calais asked, patting him on the back.

Basin hugged her knee.

"About a week," he shouted.

"No you weren't."

"I promise."

"What did you eat then?"

Basin scratched his cheek.

"Opossums and flowers."

Calais scrunched her face.

"Yuck," she said.

"Yuck," Basin repeated.

A Doppler effect and Basin twirled around, dizzying himself.

"Not wise, short sweet."

"Iowa," Basin said.

"What?"

"Ice cream," Basin said.

Calais crouched down, and Basin clasped onto her back.

They met the ice cream truck on a corner of South Main Street, about a block away from their home—a string of hypnotized children, and Basin could recognize their looks of anticipation of joy, in a way almost making him encounter a feeling of melancholy. Basin tugged on Calais' hand and pulled her aside.

"Dodo."

"Hey, we're out of the line, short sweet. What's wrong, little thing?"

"Let's wait, Dodo."

"How come?"

Basin looked at the children who were standing in line behind them—picking and choosing and pointing at the pictures on the side of the ice cream truck, dreams full of splashed colors.

"I feel bad," Basin said.

"Are you feeling bad?"

Basin nodded.

"Is it your stomach or your head?"

Calais put the back of her hand against his forehead, gentle.

"Not like that, Dodo."

"Why is that, then?"

Basin looked down the road and waved at a cat who was fiddling around in a garden. A different kind of music could also be heard, mixed in with the melodies of the truck, zydeco on a Friday night. A bicyclist rode by, holding a bag from Raising Cane's—overhead, as Basin now turned his attention toward the sky, he saw a cloud of cupcakes, soothed by hues of pinks giving way to a yellow and orange bleached air—where the world ended, Basin gathered, he whispered nothing.

"I just want everyone to be happy," Basin said, playing with Calais' fingers. "Let's let them get their ice cream first and then we can get ours after them. I just want them to be happy, Dodo."

"You're a little twinkle of twilight, little thing."

And there was a twinkle in Basin's eyes, hearing the loving voice of his mother, though he didn't know what she meant. They stepped aside and watched the line of children make their way, one by one, asking for this and that, and counting out their quarters and dollars—their parents helping them out. By the time it cleared out, the sun was down and the music coming from the ice cream truck matched the stars.

"Grandie," Basin said.

He held a ten-dollar bill and looked around at all of the pictures of ice cream.

Grandie wasn't the name of the man in the truck—actually, no one knew his real name, but Grandie wasn't even his common nickname, one that everyone called him—it was only Basin who called him that. Seldom did he call anyone by their actual names.

"Hey there now, little Bass," Grandie said. "Fancy this or fancy that?"

Basin gave him a high five.

"I got it," the child said in a squeaky voice.

But before he ordered, he tugged on Calais' hand.

"What do you want, Dodo?" he asked. "Dodo—Dodo—Dodo—what do you want, Dodo?"

"Oh I'm good, short sweet. You order what you want."

"But Dodo—I can't, not until you get an ice cream, Dodo."

Moments like those led Calais to see the world in a loving way. She whispered into Basin's ear.

"Grandie," Basin said.

"Yes, sir."

"How about one Strawberry Rocket and one Fudge Fudge Delight, Grandie? Please, Grandie."

He took out two popsicles from the freezer and handed them over to Basin.

"Grandie," Basin said. "Grandie, do you have any hot sauce?"

He pretended to look around the truck—shuffling about and making clanking sounds.

"I'm all out, little Bass."

"What about Tony's? Grandie—do you have any Tony's?"

Grandie pretended to look around again.

"Sorry—young sir."

"Thanks, Grandie."

Basin gave Calais the Strawberry Rocket before trying to give Grandie the money.

"This one is on me," he said.

Another high five.

The music of the ice cream continued to play in Basin's head, hovering around in all sorts, matching the magic of his night as they walked back home.

"Which one would Dodo have gotten, Dodo?" Basin asked.

"Definitely the Fudge Fudge Delight," Calais replied without hesitation. "You two share the exact same sweet tooth."

"Sweet tooth," Basin echoed. "I like that."

He was back in the dryer—Calais sat outside on the back porch as Basin's world tumbled and tossed around, licking the popsicle with one eye closed, tilting his head this way and that.

This was Calais' favorite kind of day—those nights when she could relax in the backyard, Basin playing in the dryer, letting his own imagination rumble around. There was a time when Calais didn't know if she was going to make it. She and her boyfriend had Basin when they were both eighteen—just graduated from Opelousas Catholic—both she and Houma found themselves in a tough situation. Having strained relationships with their own parents, which was one of the reasons why she and Houma found solace in each other, bringing them close during their senior year of high school, they were on their own. Houma started off strong though during Calais' pregnancy, finding himself a job as an electrician—being quick to learn with skillful hands led him to stable income. Calais picked up shifts at the local bar—its owner, Ledet, looked after her, giving her the Friday and Saturday night shifts and the Sunday afternoon slots during football season.

With just a glance over her shoulder—just like that—Calais found herself alone when Houma died while volunteering with the fire department. During a hurricane, he had gone to help an elderly family take shelter from their trailer home, only for it to come crashing down in the winds, taking him away.

"Dodo," Houma said, just before he closed his eyes.

Using her shifts at the bar to fund her tuition at the T.H. Harris Campus, the community college led her, much like Houma, to become an electrician, which was now her profession—the town seeing her as one of the kindest, most reliable technicians in the area.

"Basin," Calais called out.

A dragonfly whirled around her head before making its way to the porch light. Basin had fallen asleep in the dryer again, his face—covered in dried chocolate from the ice cream—pressed against the gray metal of the machine. She pulled him out and carried him inside, onto the couch.

"Wake you, Basin—little thing."

She tugged on his ear.

"Hot dog," he said, yawning.

"You know it."

A plain hot dog in a bun with Tony's sprinkled on it—that was all it took for Basin to enjoy his dinner. He sat on the carpet, in front of the TV. It was off. Basin liked to watch television without it being on—pretending and imagining all that he saw on the screen, sometimes startling Calais when he giggled or shouted or jumped around with the creations in his head. Calais would sit next to him, too, looking at the blank screen and playing along with her little one.

This time—Basin was different, and there was a silence that led to this sensation of sadness as he sat in front of the blank TV screen, eating his hot dog. There were tears as Calais sat down next to him.

"Little child," Calais said. "What's wrong? What's wrong, little child?"

"I'm just watching TV, Dodo."

"What are you watching?"

"Dodo. I'm watching Dodo."

He wiped his face with his wrist, the other hand still holding the hot dog.

"Like me, Dodo or Dodo, Dodo?" Calais asked.

"Like Dodo, Dodo," Basin replied.

"What's he doing, short sweet?"

She put her hand on his back.

"He's in the attic."

Basin took a bite out of his dinner. Outside, the frogs were loud—almost as if they were generating energy for the rest of the world.

"What's he doing in the attic, little child?"

Basin turned his hot dog the other way around and bit from the uneaten end.

"He's fixing the house," he said between his chews. "He's holding all these wires, and he's connecting them, Dodo, and he's pushing switches, Dodo, and he's wearing a brown cap, Dodo."

How would he know this, Calais wondered—her son was too young to recognize that his father was an electrician, and not only that, but also that he wore a brown cap when he went to work—a hat that Calais had given to him as a gift.

"These are memories," Basin said.

"He loves you so much," Calais said, her voice in a hush.

"I know. I just miss him."

"He misses you, too. I miss him, too, little thing."

Calais kissed him on the top of his head, just where his hair parted, and just as she tapped his nose with her index finger, the power went out.

"Dodo," Basin said.

Calais looked around the living room. She leaned back and looked into the kitchen—at the microwave, which was blank—no time.

"Must be something," Calais said. "Just sit put. Finish your dinner and then stay in this room."

"I love you, Dodo."

"Oh, I love you as big as the galaxy."

That was Basin's favorite word, and Calais could see his teeth. She walked out front and there was no light.

"So it's not just us."

She looked around and didn't see any movement—the frogs echoed in her head, a dragonfly whizzed by.

"You still there, Basin," Calais called out.

"I'm sleeping in the dark," he replied.

"You keep doing that."

Inside, Calais took out her phone and there was a message notification.

It was from the City of Opelousas, a warning that there was an escape—an alert. A photo was attached to the message—someone Calais recognized from her time at the bar. He wasn't a regular but would pop in from time to time, sporadically. She remembered him to be nice, though, tips were good—a yes ma'am, thank you ma'am kind of person—clean shaven with a hint of cologne. He was handsome, Calais always thought.

"You keep sleeping in the dark, short sweet," Calais called out.

"I'm still sleeping in the dark, Dodo—I am."

Calais pulled out a baseball bat from her closet—it hadn't moved, not the slightest since Houma's death. She went to the kitchen and pulled out a steak knife—all of the other ones, she hid. A hammer in one pocket and a screwdriver in the other.

"Basin," she whispered.

"I'm pretending to sleep," he whispered back.

"Get you to the spaceship," Calais said. "Real quick—get you to the spaceship until I come get you."

She heard a shuffling and the door whine—through the window, she saw his motion, entering the dryer.

"Shut it," she whispered, hoping he'd somehow understand.

He did.

She sat in the kitchen, the bat leaning against her knee—looking through the window. Then it happened. There was a tap on the screen door—like it was in rhythm, almost in a beat which Calais once knew. She remained still, grasping the bat.

"Houma, honey—I need that electricity, dear," she whispered.

The screen door swung open—the same knock on the wooden door itself.

What is that, Calais thought—why do I know that? She remained still. The knocking continued—it was quiet, nothing rushed or loud. Calais didn't know why—she couldn't understand what made her want to, but with the bat in one hand and the knife in the other, she walked to the door, putting her ear against it. More knocking—still in rhythm.

"What?" Calais said.

A quiet voice—"I need some help, ma'am."

Ma'am.

"Are you trouble?" Calais asked, taking a step back.

"I'm not trouble, ma'am."

"I have a knife and a bat."

"I understand, ma'am."

She quietly unlocked the door and took a few more steps back.

"Come in."

The knob turned and the door creaked open—a silhouette inside a shadow, Calais thought as the man walked in.

"You can stay put right there," she said. "Just at the front."

A dragonfly flew by behind him.

"I'm hurt, ma'am."

"You're Renee, right."

"That's right."

"I know you from the bar—some time ago."

"Is that so, ma'am?"

"It's so."

Renee turned on a flashlight and shone it down at the floor, and then he turned it around to reveal his face—bloodied and ruined.

"That's not good."

"No, ma'am."

Calais couldn't stop thinking about it.

"That knock—why'd you knock like that?"

"Houma taught me."

"Houma."

"Yes, ma'am."

"What do you know about Houma?"

"He saved my life once."

Calais gave him directions as to where to shine the flashlight—toward the kitchen.

"You sit right there."

"Is Basin good?"

"He's not here."

"Yes, ma'am."

"You're in trouble, you know that, right? They'll be here soon."

"I'm sure, ma'am."

The softness in his voice, almost welcoming despite the situation, made Calais feel a bit more relaxed even though she still held the knife and the bat.

"I had to come see you," he said. "For Houma."

Calais pictured Houma's face—one big flash, a gleaming smile and a loud laugh. She missed his laugh.

"I got something for you, ma'am."

"For me?"

"For Basin, ma'am—it's from Houma."

"Now how's that—he's dead now."

"Yes, ma'am—I was there, ma'am."

Calais started to breathe hard—she was feeling dizzy.

"At the house," he continued, "I heard his last words."

Calais stumbled a bit before regaining her strength.

"Dodo," Renee said.

"Dodo," Calais said, a trace of a smile.

Renee put his hand in his pocket, which made Calais flinch, but there was nothing. He pulled out a photo and held out his hand for her to take it.

"Hold it up and shine your light on it."

Renee did as she said. Calais, with all of the strange energy inside of her, felt like she was seeing a ghost—a ghost of Houma through the photo that Renee was holding up to her. It was a picture of a galaxy—Calais remembered Houma buying the postcard from the museum, just after Basin was born.

"He wrote a note on it, ma'am—on the back. It's for Basin. He told me to give it to him five years after his funeral, if he wasn't going to make it, that is."

Renee told her that before Houma had passed away, that he always kept the postcard in his pocket in case something happened to him when he was volunteering for the fire department.

"This was such the occasion," Renee said.

It was exactly five years since Houma's funeral service, Calais remembered. She quickly grabbed the postcard and took a step back.

"I promise I'm no trouble," Renee said.

Calais believed him.

"I broke out just for this—I promise, ma'am."

"What did you do?"

"I just needed some money, ma'am—it's been tough the past few years. That's all."

Calais took in a deep breath. I miss you, Houma, she thought, but here you are, right here in my pocket—galaxy. She walked to a drawer next to the fridge and pulled out some cotton, rubbing alcohol, and gauze—all easily accessible for those days when Basin would jump off the oak in the front yard.

"Let me fix you," she said.

"Thank you, ma'am."

Renee didn't wince or fidget as he felt the sting of the rubbing alcohol or the gauze pressing against his face. Soon after she poured him a glass of water.

"Thank you, ma'am."

He drank it in one gulp—his shadow, almost like a life in its own, vibrated against the wall from the shine of the flashlight. Calais' hands trembled.

"You should get," she said. "I'd gather they're all out and about looking for you."

"No need, ma'am—I'll be going back. I just wanted to keep my promise. That's all."

"You take care of yourself."

Calais' own shadow—the core of her body, hesitant in its breathing against the kitchen tiles.

"Thank you, Renee," she said.

With a click, he was gone.

When Calais walked out to the dryer, she heard Basin laughing. The air was dark—an unusual quiet of the town settled in—just Basin and his laughter. She knocked on the door.

"You're still awake now, aren't you, sugar?"

"Dodo—Dodo—good night, Dodo."

"We'll get you back inside, short sweet, but I have a photo for you—a postcard from far, far away."

"Dodo."

"That's right, little thing—Dodo."

Using only the glow of the moon and the tint of the stars, holding it up, Calais read Houma's message to Basin—her face, much like the morning dew to arrive in a few hours. Basin listened—he lay still in the dryer, head poked out and leaning on his mother's shoulder as her back was against the machine. As she read, the power came back on and the city hum was back intact. Calais continued on, in a low voice—deep breaths in between, lips unstable. She was able to finish, and there was a silence. A dragonfly whirled around Calais' head as Basin put his hand on her shoulder.

"Dodo," he whispered, tugging on her hair. "That's Dodo, right Dodo?"

"From far, far away, sweet short. He loves you. From far, far away."

"He's in the galaxy," Basin whispered.

Calais leaned over and kissed him on the cheek. She kept her head back and Basin twirled his body around, head still poking out of the dryer—both facing the sky, and on that night—that very strange night, Opelousas was electric.

Acknowledgments

"Frog Creek Crow" appeared in *Mid/South Anthology*; "Galileo's World" appeared in *Jabberwock Review*; "Atchafalaya Darling" appeared in *Arkansas Review*; "Opelousas Electric" appeared in *Palooka*; "The Rock And The River" appeared in *The Puritan*; "Redfish" appeared in *Cowboy Jamboree*; "A Vermilion Sad Song" appeared in *Louisiana Literature*; "The Song Of The Bark" appeared in *Vol. 1 Brooklyn*; "By the Pond Back Home" appeared in *Poverty House*; "A Familiar Frottoir" appeared in *Scrawl Place*.

Thank You

Atchafalaya Darling couldn't have been written without the support, love, and care of the following lovely beings: Thank you to my friends, who without hesitation, have always shown so much kindness and support—your friendship means so much, truly and sincerely. Thank you, Mike Bourgeois and Andy LeGoullon. Thank you, Chad and Bianca Cosby. Thank you, Karl Schott and Mandy Migues. Thank you, Luke Sonnier. Thank you, Patrick O'Neil. Thank you, Jerome Moroux. Thank you, Katie Culbert. Thank you, Story Frantzen, Abby Langford, and Jacob Camden. Thank you, James Yates. Thank you, Rien Fertel. Thank you, Sean Leon. Thank you, Casie Dodd. Thank you, Aimee Bender, for your thoughtful and kind words. Many thanks to all of the print and online journals for giving these stories a chance. Thank you, Lafayette Barnes & Noble. Many thanks to the Literary Community who has provided so much encouragement. Thank you, Belle Point Press—for all of this. To my parents, Sarmistha and Subrata Dasgupta, my brother, Deep and my sister-in-law, Heidi—I love you all so much. Thank you, always, for being there. Love.

SHOME DASGUPTA is the author of *The Seagull and the Urn* (HarperCollins India), *Cirrus Stratus* (Spuyten Duyvil), *Tentacles Numbing* (Thirty West Publishing House), *The Muu-Antiques* (Malarkey Books), *Histories of Memories* (Belle Point Press), *Anklet and Other Stories* (Golden Antelope Press), *Pretend I Am Someone You Like* (Livingston Press), *Spectacles* (Word West Press), *Mute* (Tolsun Books), *i am here And You Are Gone*, which won the 2010 OW Press Contest, and a poetry collection, *Iron Oxide* (Assure Press).

His fiction, poetry, and creative nonfiction have appeared in *McSweeney's Internet Tendency*, *American Book Review*, *New Orleans Review*, *Arkansas Review*, *New Delta Review*, *Necessary Fiction*, *Louisiana Literature*, *Jabberwock Review*, *Parentheses Journal*, *Magma Poetry*, and elsewhere. His work has been anthologized in *Best Small Fictions 2019* (Sonder Press), *Best Small Fictions 2021* (Sonder Press), *Best Small Fictions 2023* (Alternating Current Press), *The &Now Awards 2: The Best Innovative Writing* (&Now Books), and *Poetic Voices Without Borders 2* (Gival Press). He lives in Lafayette, Louisiana.

Belle Point Press is a literary small press
along the Arkansas-Oklahoma border.
Our mission is simple: Stick around and read.
Learn more at bellepointpress.com.